HARLEQUIN®
Presents

Welcome to the new collection of Harlequin Presents!

Don't miss contributions from favorite authors Michelle Reid, Kim Lawrence and Susan Napier, as well as the second part of Jane Porter's THE DESERT KINGS series, Lucy Gordon's passionate Italian, Chantelle Shaw's Tuscan tycoon and Jennie Lucas's sexy Spaniard! And look out for Trish Wylie's brilliant debut Presents book, *Her Bedroom Surrender!*

We'd love to hear what you think about Harlequin Presents. E-mail us at Presents@hmb.co.uk or join in the discussions at www.iheartpresents.com and www.sensationalromance.blogspot.com, where you'll also find more information about books and authors!

D0829961

Harlequin Presents®

They're the men who have everything—
except brides...

Wealth, power, charm—
what else could a heart-stoppingly handsome
tycoon need? In the GREEK TYCOONS
miniseries, you have already been introduced to
some gorgeous Greek multimillionaires who are
in need of wives.

Now it's the turn of beloved Presents author
Michelle Reid, with her sensual romance
The Markonos Bride

This tycoon has met his match, and he's decided
he *has* to have her...*whatever* it takes!

Michelle Reid

THE MARKONOS BRIDE

GREEK
TYCOONS

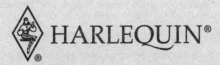
HARLEQUIN®

TORONTO • NEW YORK • LONDON
AMSTERDAM • PARIS • SYDNEY • HAMBURG
STOCKHOLM • ATHENS • TOKYO • MILAN • MADRID
PRAGUE • WARSAW • BUDAPEST • AUCKLAND

If you purchased this book without a cover you should be aware that this book is stolen property. It was reported as "unsold and destroyed" to the publisher, and neither the author nor the publisher has received any payment for this "stripped book."

ISBN-13: 978-0-373-12723-8
ISBN-10: 0-373-12723-5

THE MARKONOS BRIDE

First North American Publication 2008.

·Copyright © 2008 by Michelle Reid.

All rights reserved. Except for use in any review, the reproduction or utilization of this work in whole or in part in any form by any electronic, mechanical or other means, now known or hereafter invented, including xerography, photocopying and recording, or in any information storage or retrieval system, is forbidden without the written permission of the publisher, Harlequin Enterprises Limited, 225 Duncan Mill Road, Don Mills, Ontario, Canada M3B 3K9.

This is a work of fiction. Names, characters, places and incidents are either the product of the author's imagination or are used fictitiously, and any resemblance to actual persons, living or dead, business establishments, events or locales is entirely coincidental.

This edition published by arrangement with Harlequin Books S.A.

® and TM are trademarks of the publisher. Trademarks indicated with ® are registered in the United States Patent and Trademark Office, the Canadian Trade Marks Office and in other countries.

www.eHarlequin.com

Printed in U.S.A.

All about the author…
Michelle Reid

Reading has been an important part of **MICHELLE REID**'s life as far back as she can remember, and it was encouraged by her mother, who made the twice-weekly bus trip to the nearest library to keep feeding this particular hunger in all five of her children. In fact, one of Michelle's most abiding memories from those days is coming home from school to find a newly borrowed selection of books stacked on the kitchen table just waiting to be delved into.

There has not been a day since that she hasn't had at least two books lying open somewhere in the house ready to be picked up and continued whenever she has a quiet moment.

Her love of romance fiction has always been strong, though she feels she was quite late in discovering the riches Harlequin has to offer. It wasn't long after making this discovery that she made the daring decision to try her hand at writing a Presents book for herself, never expecting it to become such an important part of her life.

Now she shares her time between her large, close, lively family and writing. She lives with her husband in a tiny white-stoned cottage in the English Lake District. It is both a romantic haven and the perfect base to go walking through some of the most beautiful scenery in England.

CHAPTER ONE

THE atmosphere in the Markonos summer villa could not grow any cooler if an ice storm had swept down from the Arctic and in through the open terrace doors.

Eyeing his father across the width of the dinner table, Andreas Markonos delivered a cold, clipped, 'No,' with an economy that brought the shutters slamming down on his hard, handsome face.

His father ripped out a sigh of frustration. 'I do not understand you!' he muttered. 'You tell me you are ready to take full control from me and here I sit ready to hand that control over to you! So what is your problem—?'

The problem was simple in Andreas's estimation. 'I will not respond to blackmail.'

'It is not blackmail but good business sense!' the older man rapped out. 'If a man wishes to succeed in our world he must have stability in his personal life! Think about it,' he insisted. 'We make snap decisions by mobile telephone, we throw our weight around by electronic mail—we can even look our victims directly in the eye via satellite technology. There is a real danger of becoming drunk on one's own power!'

'Are you suggesting that I am drunk on power?' Andreas demanded.

'Ah—' the flick of his father's hand was dismissive '—you know very well that you shock and impress everyone with your ability to think at the speed of light,' he conceded. 'But I have been there before you, Andreas. I know how it feels to fly so high you are in danger of singeing your wings! I keep you grounded to some extent at present but who will do so when I retire?'

'Myself?'

It was like waving a red rag at a cantankerous old bull. Orestes Markonos lurched forward in his seat, his seventy-year-old world-toughened expression pinning his son with a ferocious look. 'Don't use that sarcastic tone on me, Andreas,' he warned thinly. 'You know what it is I am talking about. I had your mother and my beloved children to keep me firmly tethered to God's good earth. You merely have some very loose ties to some very loose women. It is not good enough!'

'I still will not marry again to please you,' Andreas returned coolly.

'You did not marry to please me the first time!' his father hit back. 'And Louisa was a mistake, you confessed as much yourself.'

A sudden stillness grabbed hold of Andreas, he felt it freeze the muscles in his face. Raising the heavy arc of his glossy black eyelashes, 'Never,' he incised very softly, 'have I ever said that Louisa was a mistake.'

'You were *both* too young and impetuous then,' growled Orestes, going for the compromise while clearly resenting doing it. It showed how much of his bluster was just a cover-up for his waning power in the face of his son's growing potent mental strength.

Which was why Andreas rarely allowed it to show like this. He respected the old man too much to want to make him feel the pinch of his ageing weaknesses.

This, however, was different. This subject was forbidden territory and his father knew it. No one spoke Louisa's name in his presence without feeling the icy whip of his response to it. And nobody mentioned his defunct marriage!

A hard sigh had him tossing aside his napkin and climbing to his feet. Turning, he strode across the room towards the drinks cabinet, with his lean body clenched inside the formal black dinner suit his mother always insisted her men wore when they sat down to eat dinner at home.

Home, he mused, slicing a glance around the elegant dining room belonging to an island villa that had been in the family in one form or another for as long as a Markonos had existed on this earth.

An island home he rarely visited these days. A place his father had been forced to issue what amounted to a royal summons to get him to come to at all! He'd understood what the summons had been about, of course, or he would have found a pressing excuse to be elsewhere. He had understood why his mother had politely excused herself after dinner and left the two of them alone.

His father's retirement from the fast-paced, cut-throat spin of empire-building was long overdue. It was time for the great Orestes Markonos to step aside and hand control to his oldest son.

For an unacceptable price.

'I am proud of you, Andreas,' his father fed after him.

'You are rib of my rib, blood of my blood! But if you want to walk in my shoes then I *will* insist that you find a new wife who will curtail your propensity to—'

'I am already married,' Andreas cut in as he picked up the brandy decanter.

'A situation that can be remedied quickly enough,' said the older man, tossing that legal problem to one side as if it did not count. 'My lawyers will deal with it—'

'*Your* lawyers?' As he swung round, the sudden spark to hit Andreas's dark eyes made his father add quickly,

'To make mere preliminary enquires on your behalf, of course.'

'Of course,' he turned back to the decanter, 'but not without my consent.'

The message was clear. His father hissed out his breath. 'Five years is long enough to grieve a past which cannot be altered.'

Was it? Pouring brandy into a squat crystal glass, Andreas chose to ignore that loaded comment.

'It is time for you to move on from it and build a new life for yourself on the solid foundations I am offering you here, with a good wife to help to keep you grounded—more sons!'

The final part of that recklessly tactless statement grabbed hold of Andreas's gut like a violent twist of a fist. 'Do you want one of these?' he managed to ask evenly enough.

'No!' Orestes barked out. 'I want you to listen to me! It is not healthy to lead the life you do these days! You upset your mother with it and lead me to despair!'

'Then you have my sincere apologies for upsetting you both.'

'I don't want your apology!' His father shot to his feet, five feet ten inches of sturdy Greek male in his seventh decade ready to take on his lean, muscled, beautifully constructed six-foot three-inch thirty-year-old son. 'I am still your father no matter how big you feel you are for the size of your shoes these days, so you will listen to the sense that I speak!'

'When you say something I want to hear!'

The angry rasp of his voice ripped around the elegant dining room. In the silence that thundered after it Andreas pulled in a tense, seething breath, angrily aware that any minute now his mother was going to come in demanding to know what was going on!

He decided to remove himself from the battlefield. Turning on his heels, he walked out through the doors which led onto the terrace. Behind him he heard his father throw back his chair and winced. As he stood glaring out across the villa's sweeping gardens towards the silk-dark ocean beyond, his grim glinting gaze settled on the string of ferry lights just gliding into view.

With no room for an airstrip on the island the weekly ferry provided an essential lifeline to the small island of Aristos. Within the hour, Andreas judged from a lifetime's experience, the small harbour town would be bursting with activity when the efficient transfer of cars, trucks, products and people began to take place. Two hours after that and the ferry would sail away again, leaving the island to settle back to its usual easygoing pace.

He liked it this way. He liked to know that without air access to tempt mass tourism here this small part of Greece would remain simply Greek. In the height of the summer season a few holidaymakers found their way here but they were rarely intrusive. Beautiful though the island was, it did not offer enough to hold most visitors here a full week until the ferry came back again. And if it were not for the advantages of being members of the rich and powerful Markonos family, with private helicopters to fly them in and out, even they would rarely get back here.

A sound of movement told him that his father was coming to join him.

'Louisa was—'

'My wife and the mother of my son,' Andreas put in. 'And you are mistaken if you believe that my youth or Louisa's youth made it easier for either of us to deal with what happened five years ago, because it didn't.'

'I know that, son,' Orestes acknowledged huskily, 'which is why I have left the subject alone for as long as I have.'

Fixing his attention on that string of ferry lights, Andreas had to fight to stop from spitting out something cutting because his father had not left the subject alone. He had not left it alone when Louisa had first come to live here as his young and pregnant daughter-in-law. He had not left it alone when, shrouded in grief, she had caught that ferry and left the island for good.

For the best had been the phrase Orestes had used on that occasion. *For the best* had returned each time the older man had attempted to bring up the subject of divorce.

Divorce, Andreas repeated to himself as he stared at those damn ferry lights. Now, there was a word that mocked itself. For how did you divorce yourself from the woman who'd lain in your arms night after night and *loved* you with every look and touch and soft sigh she uttered? How did you divorce yourself from the sight of her giving birth to your child?

And how did you divorce yourself from the inconsolable sight of her the day you placed that child in the ground?

You didn't. You lived with it. Night and day you lived with it. Night and day you scanned through a kaleidoscope of memories; some light, some dark, some so unbearable you wished you could switch off your head. And *for the best* became a soul-stripping insult, just as *time to move on* did. For how did you divorce yourself from all of that grief and agony and move on in your life as if it had never happened at all?

You didn't. You just *lived* with it.

'Andreas—'

'No.' Cold as ice now, he turned to put his glass down. 'This conversation is over.'

'This is madness!' the older man exploded, losing all patience. 'Your marriage is finished! Accept it! Divorce her. Move on!'

Grim features cut from rock, Andreas turned and walked down the terrace, his long stride driving him down the steps and into the gardens with the darkness swallowing him up. Two minutes later he was behind the wheel of his open-top sports car and roaring away.

He should not have come here, he told himself as he sent the car sweeping down the driveway. He should have ignored his father's summons and done what he usually did at this time of year, which was to put himself as far away from this damn island as he could!

The tense shape of his mouth bit back hard against his teeth when he was forced to stop at the road to allow an old man and his ambling donkey and cart to pass by.

Life at its most idyllic, he observed cynically. A donkey,

a cart and a bottle of ouzo stashed somewhere. A small-holding up in the hills with a homely, fat wife waiting for him, a few olive trees, some chickens and a small herd of goats to tend.

A way of life in other words, so detached from his own way of life that it was impossible to believe that he and the old man had been born on this same small Greek island at all.

Like chalk and cheese, he contrasted. Like two alien beings that happened to find themselves occupying the same patch of ground.

Like him and Louisa when he had been the arrogant twenty-two-year-old home from university for the long summer break and she had been a sweet seventeen spending six weeks with her family in a rented villa by the beach.

Six weeks that had changed both their lives forever. He had not been able to keep his hands to himself and she had been so willing to be seduced.

Stupid, blind, reckless youth, Andreas damned that mindless time in his life. They had fallen for each other like a pair of blind lemmings and taken on the whole damn opposition from two different worlds! Three years after their first meeting the two of them had grown so old that the man in his cart and his homely, fat wife would look—feel—younger now than he and Louisa had done back then.

A thick curse raked the back of his throat as he breathed it. Throwing the car into gear, he set it moving again, feeling the silken heat of the summer evening brush his face in much the same way it had done on the fateful night he had driven this same route into town. His only intention then had been to meet with his friends in a bar by the harbour where they would indulge in their favourite occupations—drinking beer and discussing fast cars and even faster women as they watched the weekly ferry come in.

He had not expected to see a leggy, long-haired blonde walking off the ferry wearing a pale blue miniskirt and a tiny top that barely covered the tender thrust of her breasts. Blue, blue eyes, he recalled, and the most amazingly smooth, creamy skin that blushed fire when she'd caught them all staring at her. She had been holding on to her younger brother's hand, lagging behind her parents because the nine-year-old boy had wanted to look at the other boats tied up at the quay.

And there he had been, Andreas remembered, already living with the arrogant belief that he was a sexual cynic, yet so blown away by the sight of her that he was left to suffer the kind of hot dreams about her which sent him out to hunt her down the next day.

His hard mouth flicked out a tense grimace. He'd found her sunbathing on the beach in front of the rented villa. It had taken them two hours to fall madly in love with each other, two weeks before they gave in to their raging desires and finally took their feelings over the edge, followed by two weeks of totally rampant, reckless loving then two weeks of *hell* once Louisa told him he'd made her pregnant.

Her parents had despised him. *His* parents had despised him—but they'd despised Louisa more.

'They think I'm a cheap little slut…'

Andreas winced at the memory of those words leaving her pain-stifled throat. Back then he could not even deny the charge because his parents *had* thought of her in that way. Her parents had seen him as an over-privileged, over-indulged, over-sexed seducer of innocent young females, but he could take their contempt because he had been indifferent to it. Louisa, on the other hand, could not take his parents' low opinion of her.

'They will come to love you as much as I do once you produce their first grandson,' he could hear himself reassuring her with all the careless arrogance of his youth.

It had been great to believe at the age of twenty-two that love could conquer everything. With hindsight and eight years to add to his twenty-two he could now positively say that if he had been forced to live in Louisa's shoes back then he would have walked away from their marriage a lot sooner than she had made her escape.

Maybe she should have run sooner. If she had run then maybe their son would still be alive now and he would have more than this *ache* he lived with night and day along with this—

He stopped the car.

Climbed out of it.

Walked away from it with his shoulders racked like iron bars.

He came to a stop at the head of the peninsula that separated the harbour town on his left from the luxury villas spread out along the coast to his right. Pushing his hands into the pockets of his black silk trousers, he honed his frowning gaze onto the string of white ferry lights once again.

Time to let go of the past and move on, his father had said. Andreas wished the hell that someone would tell him how he could make the past let go of him.

Had Louisa let it go? The question flicked like the tip of a whip across his grim features. How would he know? How the hell would he know anything about her when they'd had no contact in five years? She could be shacked up with some nice, steady Englishman for all he knew, giving him those soft, loving touches and smiles and—

His stomach muscles contracted—all of him contracted: mouth, jaw, throat, chest, loins…

Turning away from what was now threatening to eat into him, Andreas wrenched at his tie as he walked back to the car. The strip of dark silk slid from around his shirt collar and landed on the passenger seat. He followed it with his jacket then flipped diamond-studded cuff-links out of his white shirt cuffs and discarded them the same way. A minute later and he was back behind the wheel and heading for town with his shirt tugged open at his brown throat and the sleeves rolled up his hair-roughened forearms, his mind grimly fixed on only one thing.

Finding a bar and getting drunk to blot out the memories.

Resting her forearms against the ferry rail, Louisa watched a set of car headlights glide over the peninsula that formed a natural barrier between the island's tiny harbour town and the more luxurious homes which lay in a scatter of twinkling lights along the side of the hill. If she looked hard enough she would be able to pick out the lights belonging to the Markonos villa—but she didn't look that hard. The villa might have been home to her once but she felt no attachment to it now.

A sigh feathered her as she leant against the ferry rail with the warm breeze gently blowing her silk gold hair back from her face. She'd been making this pilgrimage once a year for the last five years to visit her son's resting place and not once in those five years had she stepped foot on Markonos land. It was as if, once she'd left Andreas, she'd severed almost all links with the Markonos name.

Coming here simply brought her back to her son.

'OK?' a gruff voice questioned beside her.

Turning her head to look up at the tall, dark, rather handsome young man who'd come to stand beside her, Louisa saw the anxious look in his eyes and smiled.

'I'm fine,' she said. 'Don't worry about me, Jamie. I come back here too often for it to be a major stress to me.'

And time softens pain, she added silently as she turned to watch the set of car headlights disappear from view down the other side of the peninsula. It would be on its way to meet the ferry, she judged. By the time the ferry opened its doors, the tiny port would be swarming with activity, the café bars lining the waterfront alive with a festive atmosphere that traditionally hit the island once a week.

'Do you remember any of this?' she asked her younger brother.

He had been so young when they first came to this island, but now look at him, Louisa thought fondly as he dipped his long body so he could rest his forearms on the rail beside her own. The scrawny little boy with a thatch of blonde hair had grown into a male hunk—youthful-style. And his hair was no longer blonde but dark and cropped to suit the current fashion, his attractive face trying its best to shed the last of its baby softness that still lingered around his cheeks.

'I remember standing right about here with you to watch as we rounded the hill,' he murmured.

'You mean you were hanging over the rail in excitement,' Louisa teased him. 'I was so scared you were going to topple over and fall in the water that I had a death grip on the waistband of your jeans.'

Jamie grinned, all flashing white teeth and man-boyish charm. 'Mum and Dad were no use. They'd caught the holiday bug and were too busy canoodling further along the rail to notice if we both fell in the water.'

Louisa's blue eyes widened. 'You remember that?'

The grin changed to a grimace. 'I remember too much about that time if you want the truth. Like you meeting Andreas and flipping your lid over him then all the craziness that followed which ended up with you being abandoned here.'

'I was not abandoned!' Louisa protested.

'Our parents abandoned you, to the Greek family from hell.'

'That's just not true—'

'Then Andreas abandoned you.'

'Because he had to finish his degree,' Louisa pointed out.

'Because he got you pregnant,' Jamie said bluntly, 'was forced to marry you then ran away—the coward.'

'Jamie!' his sister gasped out. 'I always thought you *liked* Andreas!'

'I did,' he shrugged, 'until he messed you up then threw you out of his life.'

'He did not throw me out of anything,' Louisa denied, shocked that he was saying any of this. 'I left Andreas of my own free will. And I would love to know, Jamie, why on earth you invited yourself along on this trip if you still feel so bad about what happened back then!'

Straightening away from the rail, her brother shoved his hands into the pockets of his low-slung baggy jeans.

'For Nikos,' he said. 'I wanted to pay my respects to Nikos and I knew I wouldn't get another chance for years once I go to uni and…' he pulled in a deep breath '…and I'm looking forward to coming face to face with Andreas so I can punch him.'

Louisa couldn't help it—she laughed. 'He would kill you before you lifted your fist to him,' she mocked. 'Have you forgotten he's six feet three inches tall and built like a tank?'

'I've been working out,' her brother said stiffly.

'For this chance to punch Andreas?'

'No,' he shifted uncomfortably, knowing that his sister knew that he'd been working out purely and simply to impress the girls, 'but I would still love the chance to have a go at him.'

'Because you believe you have—what right?'

His chin thrust forwards. 'The right of a brother who never did understand why Dad didn't beat the hell out of Andreas years ago when he left you in the state you were in.'

Grief-stricken, in other words, Louisa recalled bleakly, so inconsolable Andreas had taken himself out of her presence to work out his own grief elsewhere. When she had finally given in to pressure and let her parents take her back to England with them, she'd expected Andreas to come and get her but he never had…

Shaking her head, she stopped herself from going down that particularly bumpy pathway. To recall how she'd eventually run back to him, only to discover *how* he had found his own form of consolation, was a fool's game, she told herself.

'Well, you are out of luck because Andreas won't be here,' she informed her brother. 'His mother's email said he's in Thailand. And since this trip here is about Nikos not

Andreas,' she then added curtly, 'I would prefer it if you kept your vengeful thoughts to yourself.'

With that she spun back to the ferry rail, frowning and wondering why she had bothered to defend Andreas when he had turned out to be such a rat, a wimp, a useless, faithless—

Beside her Jamie shifted his stance. 'Sorry,' he mumbled.

'Look,' she said quietly, 'we're turning into the harbour…'

Sure enough, the ferry was nosing round the headland and the town, with its pretty whitewashed tumble of buildings hugging the curving hillside, was floating into view. Lights from the line of open-air café-bars glowed softly in the warm night and the sound of Greek music drifted across the still water, welcoming them in.

The warm breeze tried its best to soothe the savagery out of his face as Andreas drove down the hill into town, the gold strap to his watch glinting against his hair-roughened wrist as he passed beneath lamplights that lit the narrow streets. As he swung the car onto the road which ran alongside the harbour the familiar sound of Greek music floated towards him from the row of café-bars lining the other side of the street.

The ferry had beaten him in, he saw as he crawled at a snail's pace, hunting for a parking space in a street lined nose-to-nose with every kind of vehicle imaginable. As luck would have it, an old truck pulled out of the line of parked vehicles and he shot into the vacant space, switched off the engine then just sat back in his seat with the brooding darkness of his gaze fixed on the flow of people trailing down the ferry companionway along with the usual offload of trucks and cars.

He did not know why he was still sitting here instead of heading for one of the bars as he had promised himself. He didn't even know why he had come into the town at all. That blazing desire to find a bar and get drunk had been an impulse, he admitted, borne on the back of an old solution to memories he did not want to face. But it had been many years now since he'd drowned his sorrows in alcohol. These days he preferred to immerse himself in work and—

His thoughts suddenly ground to a standstill. His heart did the same thing, every muscle he possessed locking up tight as his eyes fixed on the young woman walking off the ferry with the warm breeze gently lifting the silk gold of her hair back from the softly pointed shape of her face.

A face he would not forget in two lifetimes. A face that had been haunting him for five long years.

It was Louisa. Louisa was walking off the ferry wearing loose white trousers and a pale blue T-shirt.

She's come home, was the next thought to hit.

Jamie had taken charge of their two canvas holdalls. Having hitched her backpack onto her shoulders, Louisa had taken charge of her brother's backpack then they'd joined the steady stream of people making their way off the boat.

It was good to reach solid land again but the smell of burning diesel fumes as the roll-on roll-off process went on around them made them hurry to reach cleaner air.

'I need to put some credit on my mobile,' Jamie announced as soon as they reached a clear patch of concrete close to the street. 'Do you think one of those bars will sell top-ups?'

'This might be a lazy backwater of a place but I think

it knows about cell-phones,' his sister said drily. 'Try the bar opposite,' she suggested. 'But I thought you topped it up before we left England?'

Her brother suddenly looked truculent. 'I've already used most of it up texting my friends.'

'Dump the bags next to me,' she told him. 'Kostas hasn't arrived to collect us yet, so I'll wait for you here.'

'Right.' Placing the two heavy bags at her feet, her brother suddenly reached out to engulf her in a bruising bear hug. 'Sorry about before. I didn't mean to upset you.'

'I know you didn't.' Louisa pressed a quick forgiving kiss to one of his cheeks. 'Now go.'

With a grin Jamie strode off, his mood back to its normal buoyancy, leaving Louisa to push a floating strand of hair from her cheek while she glanced down the street, looking for the silver Mercedes that belonged to the Markonos family. The only concession she made to still being a Markonos was that she never came here without first alerting her mother-in-law so that Isabella could then confirm that Andreas would not be here.

Not that she ever expected to see him. In truth, she suspected that Andreas was made aware of her visits here so that he could stay well away.

Crazy situation, she thought with a sigh as she placed Jamie's backpack on top of the larger bags then stripped off her own. Was Isabella afraid she was going to throw herself at her precious son all over again if they ever did happen to meet?

More to the point, did Andreas fear it?

Straightening up, she sent another flickering glance up and down the busy street, looking for Kostas. It wasn't like the old family retainer to be late. Usually he was parked in prime position with the boot of the car already—

It was then that she saw him and her mind suddenly emptied, everything spinning right out of focus for a few dizzying seconds before it spun violently back into focus again on his tall, dark, very still stance.

He was standing less than six feet away, leaning against an open-top sports car. Bright white shirt, black trousers, lustrous dark skin. Her heart gave a wild leap against her ribs then just rolled over and over. For the next few dizzy seconds she tried hard to convince herself it was not really him. It was impossible, she told herself. He was in Thailand. She was dreaming him up because her row with Jamie had planted his image in her head!

Then he moved, flexing those wide shoulders inside the white shirt as he straightened away from the car's shiny black bodywork with the old well-remembered smooth animal grace. Heat poured a burning hot trail down her front. It was physical, it was sexual, it was breathtakingly familiar.

'Andreas,' she breathed on the thick shaken whisper.

'Louisa,' he returned huskily.

CHAPTER TWO

THE rough silk texture of his voice played across her flesh in a complicated mix of pain versus pleasure. Shocked, she felt tears suddenly sting at her throat. Her mouth even wobbled. She had to push a hand up to cover it.

Something blazed in his eyes and he took a step forward only to pull to a stop again, tension singing from every taut sinew as he sent his gaze swinging across the street to the bars.

When he looked back at her the blaze had cooled to black ice. 'What the hell is going on?' he raked at her.

Louisa blinked, unable to make sense of the angry question. Did it mean that he was as shocked to see her standing here as she was to see him?

Dragging the hand from her mouth, 'W-we've just arrived on—on the ferry—'

'I saw,' he bit out. 'So who is the good-looking toy boy you brought with you?'

Toy boy? Did he mean Jamie? She let out a thick laugh. 'But surely you—'

A loud noise coming from directly behind her suddenly grabbed her attention. Twisting her head, she didn't get a chance to finish what she was saying before a group of people were almost on top of her and she was being jostled in their eagerness to head across the street to the bars. One of them gave her a hard nudge in the back, pushing her forwards. With the bags still sitting heavily at her feet she found she had nowhere to go. A startled cry left her lips as she began to topple forwards, her hands shooting out with an instinctive need to break her fall.

The next thing she knew a pair of hands had clamped around her waist and she was being lifted right off the ground and over the top of the bags. Her fingers closed around taut male biceps. Her cheek brushed against a tense parted mouth. She looked up—he looked down. How Andreas had managed to move so fast she would never know but as fresh shock merged with the tight sizzle of awareness that spun up through her body a soft gasp left her strangled throat.

Mou theos! Andreas cursed inwardly as her warm breath brushed across his mouth. Her familiar scent raked over his senses, the feel of her slender shape in his hands made the beat of his heart accelerate. She fitted against him as if she belonged there and for a few twisting, taut seconds all he wanted to do was to wrap her even closer and kiss—kiss—*kiss* the hell out of her.

Or strangle her.

His mood was that hairline it could take him either way! He was angry. What the *hell* did she think she was doing bringing another man here to this island?

'OK?' he rasped once he'd let her feet touch sure ground again.

Her quivering mouth parted on a breathless little, 'Yes—th-thank you,' said so very politely it snapped his lips into a biting, tight line.

She tried to take a step back from him but the bags were now firmly planted against the backs of her heels, forcing him to re-establish his grip on her when she almost toppled backwards, his long fingers splaying out around her narrow ribcage, his thumbs daring to move in a sweeping arc that settled them just beneath the warm thrust of her breasts.

She was wearing no bra. The knowledge stung him. She was still so slender his hands could almost span her. Still so physically fragile he could snap her in two. And the latter prospect was definitely winning at this precise moment because she had come here to *his* island with another man *and* she was wearing no bra beneath the skimpy vest-top!

Louisa needed to breathe but found that she couldn't. She needed to put some space between them—in fact it was critical that she did so because her senses were confused enough by this meeting without having to endure his intimate touch as well!

And she did not want her senses confused. It was over between them. The link, the union had been broken a long time ago.

'Please take a step back,' she instructed unsteadily.

To her relief he did as she bade, removing his hands from her body and taking that vital step backwards. The reprieve from his closeness sent a violent quiver shooting through her as she unclipped her fingers from his arms and slid them away too.

Then the tension came back, an ear-screeching silence. Louisa stared at the jostling crowd talking loudly in a foreign language she did not recognise as they swarmed across the street, eager to eat and drink before they had to return to the ferry before it sailed away to its next destination. For a wild moment she wanted to flee herself.

She did not want to be standing here with Andreas. She did not want to look at him at all! She had been so very careful over the years to make sure that it didn't happen, now she felt awkward and vulnerable and…

Oh, where was Jamie? Where was Kostas? Tugging in a tense breath, she took a quick look around.

'Your lover is having to queue,' Andreas said harshly.

Swinging her gaze back to him, she caught the full icy blast of his anger. Her own anger snapped to the fore. 'He's not my lover,' she denied, 'and if you just let me—'

'Whoever he is, you had no right to bring him here.'

So loftily stated—a Markonos declaration in every which way she wanted to take it because they always did believe they were the ruling gods here.

'Your family does not own this island, Andreas,' Louisa hit back furiously. 'I can visit here with whomsoever I please! And if you just let me finish what I keep trying to tell you then you would know by now how stupid you are going to feel when I—'

'Your navel is showing.'

As a brain-stopper it worked like a dream. Beginning to feel very confused and a little disoriented, much as though she'd stepped off the ferry straight into a nightmare, Louisa glanced down.

The sizzling spit of his anger held Andreas imprisoned as he followed her gaze to the narrow band of creamy, smooth flesh left bare by the low-cut style of her trousers. When his mouth began to moisten he tightened his lips back against his teeth, further infuriated that his memory bank seemed perfectly happy to feed him the sensation of tasting the perfect oval laid bare for anyone to see!

She hitched up the low-cut trousers.

He could not stop himself from making a taut, restless shift of his stance. Mad feelings were running riot inside him—the residue of shock from seeing her walk off the ferry, a gut-stirring awareness of how breathtakingly beautiful she still was. How had he managed to let himself forget that? How the hell had he gone five long years without his head reminding him of what it was about her that had driven him crazy over her in the first place?

He did not have the answer but for those first few shock-rolling seconds as he'd followed her progress off the ferry he'd sat behind the wheel of his car and been tossed right back into an eight-year-old pot of hot, bubbling lust! Until he'd noticed the man walking behind her, seen the ease with which she'd disappeared into his arms before the guy had shot off across the street.

His wife—his *wife*, cavorting in public with another man right here on *his* island, where everyone knew who she was and what had happened between them.

His gut ripped him in two and he swung his back to her at the same time that she swung away from him. Tension sang between them, anger, a bright, burning antagonism that made even less sense than everything else he was feeling right now.

'Much you know about backwaters,' a new voice intruded on the grinding atmosphere. 'They don't do top-ups in the bars over there, so I'm going to have to wait until tomorrow to find a bank or a hole-in-the-wall and…'

Jamie's dry tone slid into silence when he saw Andreas.

Louisa watched helplessly as her brother's face closed up like a drum. After the words they'd exchanged on the ferry she had no idea how he was going to react once the shock had worn off at having his main target standing right here.

'S-say hello to Andreas, Jamie,' she prompted warily.

What he did was stiffen up like a soldier.

'Jamie…?' Andreas swung round. Surprise hit his lean features then he pushed out a laugh. *'Mou theos*, so it is!'

Andreas stepped forward to offer her brother a friendly hand in greeting. Louisa caught her bottom lip between her teeth as she waited for Jamie to respond. He didn't take the hand but shifted his gaze from her face to Andreas. A different kind of tension suddenly pulsed in the warm evening air. She saw the slight stiffening in Andreas's long spine as he stood there with his hand still determinedly outstretched and she knew he'd caught on to Jamie's frame of mind. Fresh silence sang like an out-of-tune melody and Louisa felt her heart begin to pound. The last thing she needed right now was for her brother to turn macho and try to carry out his threat.

'Jamie,' she breathed helplessly.

With a reluctance she felt creep all over her skin like a shiver, Jamie finally found some stiff manners and took the offered hand. For the next few minutes Andreas joined the younger man in conversation, forcing answers to the questions he put to him with a smooth aplomb that showed up the differences in maturity between them.

When Jamie eventually excused himself to go and stash his wallet in his backpack, Andreas turned to her. 'I owe you an apology,' he said gruffly.

'Not really.' She sent him a brief tense smile. 'He has changed an awful lot since you saw him last.'

The fact that she was letting him off for being so down-right arrogant and loathsome to her didn't seem to impress him much because he flattened his mouth into that thin, flat line again.

Then he changed the subject. 'Presumably you are staying with my parents at the villa,' he said briskly, only to add grimly, 'It is a shame they did not see fit to warn me you were coming then maybe this—'

'We're not—'

'Not what?' He frowned down at her.

'We're not staying at the villa,' she provided, saw a complete lack of comprehension stamp itself onto his lean, hard features and struggled to hold back a sigh.

Shifting her weight from one foot to the other, she slid her eyes away from him and tried to decide what the heck she was supposed to say next. She was in no doubt that Andreas had been as surprised to see her standing here as she had been to see him, which had to mean that his mother had not been possessed with a sudden urge to confess her complicity in keeping her trips here a secret from her son. And if Isabella was maintaining her silence then Louisa had no wish to drop her mother-in-law in it by blurting out any stupid hints.

It was then that she saw Kostas standing by the silver Mercedes now parked a few car spaces down from where they stood. Her heart kicked out of rhythm. The old family retainer's expression was guarded to say the least. Kostas wasn't sure what to do next. Well, join the club, she thought drily.

'We thought you were in Thailand,' her cool-toned brother announced.

'Thailand,' Andreas repeated, his eyes narrowing on Jamie. 'An—interesting mistake to make,' he murmured ever so softly.

Louisa closed her eyes on a silent curse because that silken tone told her things she did not want to hear. One thing she could never call Andreas was slow on the uptake once all the clues started falling into place—Thailand had just become a very big clue.

When she opened her eyes again Andreas was looking directly at her and his eyes had narrowed even more. A tight flutter took up residence in her chest and she swerved her attention to Jamie.

'Kostas has arrived,' she murmured, waving a horribly shaky hand towards the old man standing by the silver Mercedes. 'W-will you stash our things in the car?'

It was like balancing on a knife-edge, she thought. Flashing glimpses of steely expressions kept lancing her way. Jamie was reluctant to move and leave her alone with Andreas. Andreas had swung round to look at the old family retainer, now he was looking back at her and his expression had turned cold. Tension zipped around all three of them and on a hot Greek summer evening she suddenly felt so chilled her flesh grew goose-pimples.

Then her brother bent and with a jerk he picked the bags up. There was no missing his mood, no misunderstanding the look he flicked at Andreas before he strode away. She and Andreas both watched in thrumming silence until Jamie reached Kostas.

Then, 'Would you like to explain to me what is going on?' Andreas drawled.

'Not really.' With a rueful honesty she knew didn't help

the situation one tiny bit, Louisa ended up adding another sigh then straightened her shoulders and made herself look up at him. 'I'm here to visit Nikos.'

Hearing their son's name spoken between them for the first time in five years locked the muscles in his dark golden features so tightly a thick lump formed in her throat so she couldn't breathe.

They both broke eye contact at the same time.

'I had already gathered that,' he returned without any noticeable inflexion in his voice. 'While I was supposed to be safely out of the way in—Thailand, I think your brother said?'

'You know he did,' she responded edgily.

'Which, to hazard a rough guess, brings my parents into this.'

Irritated now, 'You don't have to be sarcastic about it,' she snapped back at him.

'I have been set up. I will be as sarcastic as I want to be.'

He'd been set up? 'Why *aren't* you in Thailand?' Louisa demanded.

'Because I was summoned here obviously,' he replied. 'How often have you come here without my knowledge?'

There was just no way she was going to answer that one. 'It's getting late,' she hedged instead, flicking a blind glance at her wrist-watch, only to frown when the time she saw did not make any sense. But then what did around here? she asked herself and dropped her wrist away. 'We need to go if we don't want to lose our rooms…'

'What rooms?' The frown came back.

It was like jumping out of the frying-pan into the fire then back again, Louisa thought heavily. 'We are staying at The Hotel.'

The Hotel being the only hotel on the island.

'Like hell you are,' he rasped. 'My wife does not reside in a third-class hotel when a ten-bedroom villa stands waiting to welcome her home!'

'Estranged wife.' It was out before she could stop it. So was, 'And the Markonos villa is not home to me any more.' Then before he could respond yet another sigh shot from her. 'For goodness' sake, Andreas, it should be obvious that I have no wish to stay at the villa. I am not here as a member of your fabulous family, I am here as myself for myself!'

'You are a Markonos,' he uttered stiffly.

I'm just not going there, Louisa decided, eyes as restless as her frazzled nerves now. 'We are staying at the hotel,' she repeated stubbornly.

'And my mother allows this?'

He just was not going to let up until he knew it all, Louisa realised and, pinning her lips together, she gave a curt nod, knowing it was way too late to keep Isabella's part in her visits here out of this.

Another silence followed—a cold, stiff Markonos silence that could freeze the blood in your veins. Her arms came up to fold across the tension packed inside her ribcage. Kostas had helped Jamie stash the bags in the boot of the car and now both of them were standing watching them and she felt a sudden urge to scream and shout and stamp her feet.

'Look,' she tried a more diplomatic approach, 'I don't…'

Andreas spun his back to her and walked away. Staring after him, Louisa wondered how she could have forgotten how overbearing he could be when the mood took him. Did he think she was finding this situation any less awful than he was? Did he think she *wanted* to be faced with her estranged husband, whose hot affairs with even hotter women had been splashed all over bright, glossy magazines for years?

He'd gone to speak to Kostas. Tall, dark, animal-lean with the potent promise of—

Oh, dear God, what was she doing? Don't go there, she told herself. Just—don't!

Taking a deep breath, she made herself track after him, noticing the way Andreas was so deliberately ignoring Jamie it was putting an angry flush in her brother's face. She arrived at the Mercedes as sets of car keys were exchanged. Kostas sent her a sheepish look then nodded politely before walking off towards the open-top sports car.

Andreas pulled open the rear door of the Mercedes. 'In,' he commanded.

Jamie immediately bristled at his tone. Needing to get this ordeal over with as quickly as she could, Louisa gave her brother a nudge and a glaring look that told him to get in the damn car.

She climbed in after him. The door shut.

'Who the hell does he think he is?' Jamie muttered.

A man who knows he's been duped by his own mother into coming here to the island and who doesn't like it. Louisa didn't blame him; she didn't like what was going on either. What was Isabella playing at?

'Shh,' she hissed at her brother.

Andreas slid into the driver's seat, the bright white of his shirt accentuating the muscular breadth of his shoulders and the rich, smooth warmth of his olive-toned skin. Louisa found herself staring at him—caught a pair of dark eyes looking right back at her through the rear-view mirror and felt pinned to the seat by an electric charge.

CHAPTER THREE

IT WAS hot, it went deep and it was bone-meltingly intimate, the dark depth of his eyes burning with a personal knowledge Louisa just hoped was not reflected in hers. She wanted to look away but found that she couldn't. Her mouth had run paper-dry, lips trembling and parting on a soundless denial that died on the tingling tip of her tongue as the years fell away in the sultry shadows separating the two of them, until she felt like that young seventeen-year-old looking at the younger man who'd so captivated her shy and vulnerable heart.

Yet he had altered more than she would have thought possible, grown so much leaner and harder as if that younger man had been carefully honed and toned during the years to present this fully matured and tougher version she was looking at now. His face had fined down, the bone structure gaining so many new angles—the high cheekbones, the ruthlessly carved shape to his jaw and his chin. His nose had never been fleshy but it had managed to slim out even more and his wide, sensual mouth that had used to flash out fabulous, sense-stealing smiles now had a grim cut to it that she didn't like to see.

Or was it finding himself faced with her again that was putting the grimness there? She didn't know, couldn't think beyond the agonising fact that he was still the most visually stunning man she had ever set eyes on, still so sensually armoured it was no wonder she was feeling as weak and susceptible as she'd always been around him.

Then she suddenly remembered how he'd looked the last time she'd seen him in their apartment in Athens, and a flash of pain hardened to a lump that lodged itself behind her ribs.

She dragged her eyes away.

As she did so the open-top sports car gave a throaty roar. Jamie glanced out of the side window to watch as the low, sleek, shiny black car made a U-turn in the street with Kostas at the wheel, and it was a mark of how angry her brother was that he could resist making a comment. He was crazy about powerful super-cars.

The Mercedes saloon came alive to a more sedate engine sound, its luxury interior almost masking the fact that the engine was running at all. It too made a neat U-turn then was gliding smoothly up the street.

The mood inside the car was not so sedate. It spat and it crackled.

This trip to Aristos was already turning into a disaster and they'd been here for less than half an hour. She dared another glance at Andreas's stern profile. Five years was a long time not to lay eyes on the man she had once loved to the point of self-destruction. In the dimness of the car's interior his lean cheek and jaw line looked even more severe than it had done a minute ago and his mouth was turned downwards slightly and tight.

What was he thinking? What did *he* suspect was going on here?

Well, she wasn't going to ask him, she determined. But she couldn't stop her eyes from drifting up to his dark hair, so fashionably cut to the shape of his head, then dropping to the span of his wide shoulders where fine shirting did very little to hide the muscular bulk beneath.

The last five years had been good to him, she acknowledged as her gaze wandered down a white shirtsleeve to the point where it had been folded back from a muscular forearm. The gold strap to his wrist-watch glinted against a strong, hair-roughened wrist, the long-fingered hand attached to it lightly gripping the leather-bound steering wheel.

Those fingers tightened suddenly, sending her eyes flickering upwards to clash with his eyes yet again. Her breathing stopped as time made that flip backwards once more and those glinting dark eyes held her totally transfixed. Thoughts started to flick between them, shared thoughts, intimate thoughts—a mutual knowledge of what made the other tick. Could he tell that she was sitting here battling to stifle a million different sensations she'd only ever felt with him?

A mobile phone began to play some weird trendy tune and Jamie dived into his pocket then began hitting buttons so he could pick up a text message.

Andreas was the first to look away this time, returning his attention to the road ahead, leaving Louisa to wilt in her seat. A few seconds later and her brother was chuckling at something, his bad mood evaporating with the help of some amusing comment one of his friends must have made. His long, rangy frame relaxed into the seat as he began spelling out his reply.

As the strangely soothing staccato beep of the phone-pad filled the silence, Louisa found her eyes drawn back to the rear-view mirror to find that Andreas was looking at her again too. They couldn't seem to stop doing it. New memories began to flow between them, the kind of memories that added a disturbing darkness to his eyes. They had used to text each other all the time with silly little things like, 'What are you doing?' 'Do you miss me?' 'I need you.' 'Why aren't you here?'

She shifted tensely on the seat. Mobile-phone technology had not been as advanced back then as it was now, especially at the beginning of their marriage, when they had used to communicate more by long-distance telephone than by text—share real conversations in which they touched with their voices to help get them through the long separations.

Duty calls, his brother Alex had used to call them. 'Our mother will have his head on a stick if he dares to miss his daily duty call to his wife.'

Alex had resented her more than the rest of the Markonos family. He claimed that she'd ruined his brother's life. 'Women fawn all over him. Do you think he's resisting their delightful temptations while you sit here growing fat with his child and he is thousands of miles away?'

She pulled her eyes away from the mirror. As she did so Andreas wondered what the hell had placed that pained look on her face.

He had—who else?

Damn the memories, he cursed silently. They were both cluttered up with them. Even her brother was suffering the knock-on effect. They had used to be good friends now Jamie looked on him as he would a poisonous snake. And it hurt. It touched something tender inside him in a place he did not want to visit because it was linked in some indecipherable way to his son.

His son… A hard lump formed in his throat as he looked at her—the mother of his lost son. She had not changed, nothing about the softly feminine shape of her beautiful face was different, the wide-spaced blue eyes, the straight little nose, the soft, full, sensational mouth she was holding tense at the moment but was still the most kissable mouth he had ever—

A sudden burn low down in his gut sent his gaze back to the dark road ahead. And he refused to look in the rearview mirror again if that was where his thoughts were going to take him.

The car sped on through the darkness, heading up the peninsula then dropping down on the other side. A few minutes later and he was making a sharp turn and diving into woodland on the dusty track which led down to the only hotel the island possessed. It had a name, though Andreas could not recall it. To the residents of Aristos it was simply The Hotel. If you did not know it was at the end of this track you would be lucky to find it, yet the sturdy, whitewashed building with its attached *taverna* sat right on the edge of one of the prettiest beaches on the island.

They came upon it now, driving out from beneath the canopy of trees onto a tiny car park lit by a single low-wattage light hanging from the canopy above the hotel entrance. Bringing the car to a smooth halt, Andreas killed the engine then climbed out. The rear doors were already being pushed open and his two passengers climbed out then stood glancing about them as he strode to the back of the car.

All around them the cicadas were calling, the warm evening air tangy with the scent of citrus and pine.

'I can hear the ocean,' Jamie said to his sister. 'Are we right on the beach here?'

So, Jamie had not made this trip before, Andreas surmised from that. Louisa answered so quietly that he lost what she said as he swung up the boot lid.

He was about to lift the bags out when Jamie came up beside him. 'I'll do that.'

'Don't be a pain, Jamie,' he said levelly, and the younger man flushed at the smooth shoot-down.

Yannis, the owner of the hotel, came hurrying out of the entrance just then to greet Louisa with warm smiles and words of welcome, only to stop dead when he saw Andreas standing there and not his old friend Kostas.

Yet more tension hit the atmosphere. Andreas ignored it as he stepped over to greet the hotel owner with a polite shake of his hand.

But Louisa knew that Andreas was aware that Yannis had stopped dead like that because he had not expected to see both of them in the same place at the same time. The island was small and the memories of its people were long. Everyone here knew how the eldest son of Orestes Markonos had fallen head over heels for a teenage tourist, made her pregnant and married her against the wishes of both families. They also knew about their son's tragic accident. They knew they lived separate lives. They knew that Andreas never came to the island when Louisa was visiting.

In quiet words of Greek he instructed Yannis to help

Jamie with the luggage. Andreas waited until they'd disappeared inside the hotel before he closed the car boot then turned to Louisa, who was still standing by the rear passenger door.

'By tomorrow we will be the talk of the island,' he drily predicted.

'So what's new there?' Louisa responded, only to instantly regret the acid in her tone. 'Sorry,' she murmured.

'Why be sorry for speaking the truth?' He came to lean against the car beside her, side-on so he was facing her, hands in his pockets—too close for comfort and placing her senses on full alert. 'I don't give a damn about what others wish to say about me.'

'You never did.' Folding her arms across her body, Louisa fixed her eyes on her flat shoes and tried not to notice how tall he seemed standing this close beside her, how big and so skin-tinglingly masculine he—

'No,' he agreed. Then he really shattered her comfort zone by lifting up a set of fingers to gently stroke her cheek. 'I was shocked out of my senses when I saw you walk off the ferry,' he confided softly. 'For a moment I thought I was dreaming.'

'Stuff nightmares are made of.' Lifting her chin up, she winged him a brief, tense smile then looked away again, dislodging his fingers at the same time.

All he did was to move the fingers to hook a stray lock of hair behind her ear. 'Not from where I was standing, *agape mou.*'

This time Louisa stiffened right away from him. 'Don't toy with me, Andreas,' she said tensely.

'I was touching, not toying.'

'You have no right to do either.'

'I feel like I do…'

That was some blunt confession to utter! 'How *dare* you say that?' She swung on him furiously.

He grimaced, the hand going back in his pocket. 'Because you are still my wife?'

Stark, cold images of what he had been doing the last time she'd seen him in their apartment in Athens sprang like a burning blister into her head. Louisa tensed away from him then used up every single one of the next ten seconds to struggle with what was now crawling around inside her, while he dared—*dared* to lean against the side of the car and watch her with that lazily mocking challenge on his too handsome face!

She lost the battle. On a seething short breath she stabbed her left hand out. 'Look,' she said, 'no gold wedding ring on my finger. No sign that I ever belonged to you at all! I use the name Jonson now—*Miss* Jonson! I do not think of myself as a Markonos any more!'

'Washed me right out of your life?' he quizzed idly.

'Yes!' she confirmed it.

He grabbed her and kissed her.

It was so unexpected that before she'd even realized what was happening he'd crushed her hard up against him and was in full, burning possession of her mouth. Lights switched on all over her body. It was that quick, that explosive, like being dragged into a seething cauldron of remembered intimacy that felt crazily as though she had never lost it at all!

Her breath caught in her throat as her lips responded, parting to his warm, moist invasion like hungry traitors to greedily invite him to do his worst. She didn't want to believe this was happening—in some wildly shocked part of her brain she was horrified that he could still do this to her, yet at the same time she was drowning in the sheer pleasure of it, lost without a shred of control. His hands had control of her body, long fingers, passionately restless, moving on her hips and her spine. He was pressing her close; she could feel stirring evidence of his passion and felt her senses stir in response.

And through it all their mouths moved on each other, hot, hungry, deeply intimate. Oh, so dreadfully intimate it came as a terrible shock when he just as suddenly pushed her back from him, making the air between them splinter with the sound of their mutual thick groans.

Holding her at arm's length, he let his fingers bite into her shoulders, eyes like glinting black lasers locked onto the swirling, shocked passion darkening her own.

Then he spoke, hard, tight, cruelly mocking. 'Not quite washed me away, *agape mou*, hm?'

The unforgivable taunt crowned her tumbling sense of degradation. She began to tremble violently. Tears stung hotly in her throat.

'Me and the thousand others,' she hit back in thick and shaking, seething disgust then pulled free of him and ran into the hotel.

Andreas watched her go and struggled to believe he'd actually said and done that.

Why had he done it? What the hell was the matter with him?

A string of tight curses raked from his tense lips as he spun around to face the car, because he knew the answer.

It lay in the million dark forces running riot inside him—not one of them fit to justify him grabbing her like that.

Her and the thousand others...

What a damn great joke, he thought bitterly, and another set of curses leapt from him as he tugged the car door open and slammed himself inside.

Still cursing, he took off from the hotel with a cruel spin of tyres.

Leaning back against the hotel doors listening to the tyres spit up gravel as the car took off, Louisa was trembling so badly she felt ready to sink into a weak, limbless huddle on the floor.

And her lips were throbbing, the hot, bitter tears that burned her eyes threatening to spill. How could he do that? How *could* he have just grabbed her and kissed her like that?

A shimmer of something horrendously desperate went riddling right through her. It settled like a sting between her thighs and on the tips of her breasts.

'You OK?'

The sound of Jamie's uncertain tone dragged her gaze to her brother. 'I'm f-fine,' she lied, fighting to pull herself together.

He did not look convinced. 'Did he say something to upset you?'

'No,' she lied yet again. 'We—we're both suffering from shock, that's all.'

But there was a lot more than shock rattling around inside her, Louisa had to admit hours later when she was still pacing her bedroom too shaken up to think beyond the whole face-to-face meeting with Andreas followed by that kiss and the humiliating way she'd fallen into it without a fight.

'Oh, give me strength,' she groaned as a flood of heat pooled low down in her abdomen, taunting her with her own wildly uncontrolled response.

How could she have done that? She couldn't still want him. She didn't *want* to still want him! Wrapping her arms around her body, she paced over to the window to stare out at the velvet-dark night. It was late and the old-fashioned double bed standing behind her should have been inviting, but each time she so much as glanced at it her stupid imagination conjured up an image of him lying there naked and waiting for her like a terrible guilty wish and—

With a jerk she took herself off to the tiny bathroom and switched the shower on. Ten minutes later, shivering with cold and grim determination, she dived between the cool linen sheets and told herself to get over that stupid kiss and go to sleep.

Andreas lounged on a chair on the terrace, the glittering darkness of his gaze fixed on the silk dark night. In front of him on a table stood the decanter of brandy and a large pot of strong coffee keeping warm on a burner.

He had changed his mind about getting drunk tonight.

His recent conversation with his parents had been short and pithy, his father's only saving grace being that he had not known Louisa was on the ferry when they'd had their after-dinner *chat*.

His mother had been a different matter. Her lack of apology in the face of his anger had been nothing short of defiant. 'I have to admit that I did not intend for you to just bump into each other as you did,' she'd admitted. 'But I did intend to make it happen before you flew off again. It is time,

Andreas, that the two of you faced each other. Now perhaps you can both bring some kind of closure to your marriage.'

'You set this up because you expect closure to result from it?'

'What else? I am tired of watching you drift through the years in a state of marital limbo. It has to stop.'

Well, limbo was not where he was right now. He was angry, on Louisa's behalf, that she had been subjected to this. He was angry for himself. He was perfectly happy with the way he ran his life. He did not want *closure*. He *liked* to recall what a lousy husband he had been. It helped to keep his emotions locked up tight.

Not so you would notice, mocked a voice in his head. You might be an emotional desert with every other woman you've known but one look at Louisa and you're spinning right off the emotional planet!

And that was the reason why he was sitting here drinking brandy and strong black coffee. The brandy was the method by which he meant to numb what was flying around inside him, the coffee the means by which he aimed to keep himself awake while he did it so that by tomorrow he would have himself back in control. Then he would visit Nikos before flying away from here, he determined, leaving Louisa to commune with their son without his interference or fear of being grabbed and kissed by the man she clearly despised.

She'd kissed him back.

Her soft mouth had parted and she'd pressed in against him and it had been like—

Cursing as something hot went spurting through his blood, Andreas got up to pace the length of the terrace then back again.

What the hell was the matter with him? They'd been separated for five years! Had not set eyes on each other once in those five years! She had walked away from this island without offering him so much as a phone call to warn him she was going to go back to England, or to give him a chance to—

'Damn,' he cursed as he glared at the disappearing ferry lights and wished he could control what was happening to him. He was thirty years old now—a mature and sophisticated man! Yet he felt as fired up as that lusty twenty-two-year old had felt the night he first laid eyes on her.

Which said—what to him?

'Ouch,' Louisa choked as she caught the open toe of her sandal on an unseen stone and almost tripped up.

What other idiot would decide on impulse to go for a walk in the middle of the night? she railed at herself as she lifted up her foot to rub the bruised end of her big toe.

And how far had she come from the hotel since she started out on this crazy venture? With only a slithery moon hanging low in the sky, it was difficult to tell. When all of that hot, senseless restlessness had sent her creeping out of bed and eventually out of the hotel, she'd only intended to take a brisk walk down the beach. How she had ended up going as far as to strike out on one of the many narrow pathways scoured into the hillside by hundreds of years of grazing goats she had no idea.

Yes, she did, she then argued with herself. She'd decided that if she couldn't sleep she might as well watch the sun come up. She'd intended to walk as far as a plateau of rock she had used to like to sit on to watch the sky slowly turn from navy blue to rich vermilion to a soft azure blue.

Her teeth buried themselves in her bottom lip when it suddenly occurred to her that it wasn't even coming light yet. Could she have got her timing all wrong? Putting her foot back on the ground, she squinted at her watch but it was too dark to read the tiny silver face.

A sigh shook her. She really should turn back.

But she didn't want to turn back.

She did not want to be alone in that hotel bedroom tormenting herself with things she had no right to feel any more! Being out here was different because while she was using up energy she wasn't thinking. She wasn't scared for her safety—not on this tiny island where the people were more honest and upright and true than a monastery of monks!

But standing on a rough-hewn hillside while it was still dark was beginning to feel just a bit spooky. If anyone happened to catch her skulking around they were going to think that she was a bit spooky too.

A soft giggle broke from her. It was crazy to do it but she suddenly saw the humour of it, the total juvenile silliness of being out here at all!

Then something warm touched her shoulder and she let out an ear-piercing shriek. It was a bat—a bat! she told herself, spinning around to check out that theory, only to have the breath fly from her body when she found she was staring at the tall, dark figure of a man dressed in ghostly grey.

CHAPTER FOUR

ONE of her hands shot up to press against her chest where her heart was hammering. 'Andreas!' she gasped out. 'You scared the life out of me!'

'My apologies,' he said.

He was standing barely two feet away from her but how he'd managed to get that close without her hearing him was enough to send cold shivers chasing up and down Louisa's spine.

'What are you doing out here?' he demanded. 'Are you out of your mind, Louisa, to be walking about on your own at three-thirty in the morning?'

Three-thirty? 'I thought it was four-thirty,' she mumbled, dragging her hand away from her pounding chest to take another look at her watch. She still couldn't read the tiny silver face but a sinking feeling inside was telling her she must have reset it to the wrong time as she'd flown in to Athens yesterday.

'Does an hour make a difference? It is still dark out here!'

'It does to the dawn,' she murmured faintly. 'I wanted to watch the sun come up.'

The way he pulled in a deep breath told her he did not

think that an adequate excuse. But she'd always loved to watch the sun rise and set in Greece; surely he must remember that?

'So what's your reason for being out here?' Looking up, she all but threw the question at him. Then another thought hit her. 'You haven't been following me, have you?'

'Oh, yes,' he ground out. 'I spent the night camped outside your window, waiting for the moment you would decide to do something as stupid as this.'

His sarcasm hit the spot it was meant to. Stuffing her hands into the baggy pockets of her white cotton trousers, Louisa snapped her lips together and glared down at her sandaled feet. The raw tension flitting between them was suffocating, the rumbling tumble of emotions put there because of that totally uncalled for, totally unwarranted—

'I was running,' he pushed out.

Running, she repeated to herself and at last took notice of what he was wearing, resentful blue eyes shifting from her feet to his. His running shoes were old and scuffed. Grey cotton jogging bottoms covered his long, powerful legs, with telling sweat marks darkening the fabric in certain places, especially around the tightly packed bowl of his hips, where—

Mouth paper-dry, she dragged her gaze upwards. He was still panting a little from his run up the hill and she felt the full visual impact of his hard male torso trapped inside a damp grey T-shirt that clung so tightly it could pass for skin.

'On the beach,' he added, and she missed his new husky tone as her eyes clung to the moisture glossing his strong brown throat. Her tongue snaked out. There was a sudden tense movement of his muscular breastplate which dragged her eyes down to it.

'I was on the way back to the villa when I saw you stumble ahead of me on the path— Stop looking at me like that, *agape mou*,' he said abruptly. 'It is dangerous…'

Startled, she flicked her eyes back to his. He wasn't laughing. He wasn't even being sardonic. Every nerve-end in her body grew stretched and tense. Tugging in a breath, she felt a flush of colour rush into her cheeks and wanted to drag her eyes away from him but she couldn't because this warm, dark, very physical man was the whole reason she'd made the impulsive decision to walk out at this ridiculous time of the night! She had not been able to lie in that bed without thinking about him being there with her.

Dear God, she thought helplessly. What a confession to make.

'I'll go back…' Jerking into movement, she sidestepped around him.

'I will walk with you.'

'I don't want you to.'

'It was not a request, *yineka mou*,' he said coolly.

'I am not your wife!' she flicked out.

'What are you, then?'

The heck if she knew, Louisa thought angrily. Not his wife, not free and single…

Pinning her lips together, she refused to answer and just took off down the slope, walking quickly—carelessly—because she needed to get as far away from him as she could before she did something really stupid and told him what was—

The hand closing around one of her wrists pulled her to an abrupt standstill. 'Don't be more foolish than you have been already,' Andreas said harshly. 'This path is treacherous.'

Panicked—spooked beyond any sight of reason because she knew what was going to happen next and that it was her own crazy weakness that was driving it—Louisa tried to wrench her captured wrist free. When he refused to let go of it she made the big mistake of swinging round to glare at him. Her troubled little world tilted as she took in his full six feet three inches of lean, sleek, muscular height. The eyes, the hair, the fabulous bone structure, the gorgeous, gorgeous sensual mouth. His hair was damp— spiked, like the eyelashes that framed his glinting dark eyes and the few curls of hair she could see clustered around the V-neck of his shirt. Trickles of sweat were still trailing down each taut cheek and the strong column of his neck and her tongue moistened with a desire to reacquaint herself with its clean, salty taste.

'Please,' she begged in a low, husky groan as the breath came and went from her body, the darkness surrounding her beginning to thicken with a new sultry heat.

'Louisa…' he breathed tensely. 'Don't do this.'

He knew what was happening to her. The glitter in his eyes and the taut set of his mouth told her so and she choked out a small whimper because she knew it was already too late. She should *not* have looked at him. She should not have let him see what was tormenting her! Knowledge brought intimacy and intimacy brought a complete collapse of all that was sensible and sane the way it had with that kiss they'd fallen into at the hotel.

'I have to go…' She tried to pull free again, desperation making her voice shake.

He muttered something in Greek then pulled her towards him. She felt the full burning heat of him as she made impact with his chest. She looked up, was instantly trapped by dark eyes swirling with an angry glint. She watched his damp brown throat move up and down as he swallowed before his tense lips parted so he could speak.

But she didn't want him to speak. She didn't want him to say anything. She just wanted to—

On another choking groan she gave in to what was driving her and reached up to hook a hand around his neck so she could bring his mouth down onto hers because *that* was what she wanted him to do with that sensual mouth!

Sensation flashed across her senses. It had been bad enough the first time when they'd kissed in the hotel car park; this time she just did not have a single ounce of control. She wanted him. She'd *always* wanted Andreas! He was a cross she had to bear because he was her first love, her only love—who really knew what made her this vulnerable to him?

Who knew what made her cling to and kiss him with a wild, hot, begging urgency that drove her tongue between his lips and sent her eager body arching into the hardness of his? All she did know was that it took only seconds for the whole thing to make the giant leap back through five years to a place in time when this explosive kind of passion had been normal to them.

The clean, damp smell of him permeated all around her. It was so exciting she just couldn't keep still. When his hands made a compulsive slide down her body she dragged her mouth away so she could lick that warm, salty gloss from his throat and heard him hiss out something very rude.

Then he sent his hands thrusting up beneath her T-shirt, stroking her smooth naked back, and pressed her even closer. His heart was thundering, the bowl of his hips filling with that potent force that made her cling all the more desperately to him. She could not get close enough, could not taste enough of him.

With a fevered whisper of, 'I want you,' she went back to his mouth.

He took the kiss over and lost them both in the pleasure of it, the hungry stab of their tongues growing greedier and more demanding as the whole thing rushed on. Maybe the darkness helped, the feeling that they were alone in the world as they stood there on the side of the hill.

Then it was gone.

Andreas was the one to stop it. He was the one to push her away from him yet again. He was the one to spin his back to her while all Louisa could do was to stand there gasping and trembling with shock at the loss.

'If you want sex that badly, then I am more than happy to provide it,' he rasped out, twisting back to catch her pained flinch. 'But not here on a dusty track, rutting like a pair of goats.'

'Why not?' Louisa challenged shrilly. 'It was pretty close to how it happened the first time between us. You did not seem so picky then!'

Something flashed across his eyes. At first she thought it was a cruel type of cynical amusement, then she realised that it was pure, glinting rage. She'd touched a nerve she hadn't even known he possessed and suddenly she'd been grabbed and pulled back against him again.

'You want to re-enact our first time?' he raked down at her. 'You want me to roll you down on the ground and lose my head again, reintroduce you to what it is like to have sex with a man out of control?'

'No,' she whispered, horribly aware that this was all her fault. 'I'm s-sorry…I don't know what came over me. I—'

'*I* came over you. Want came over you. Need—*lust*. A sudden desire for sex with your hot-blooded Greek!' His contempt whipped her skin. 'I must therefore assume that your last five years in the sexual company of Englishmen has not been enough to satisfy you.'

'And what's your excuse?' she hit back at the cruel-tongued brute. 'What drove you to respond as you did? A sudden desire to re-enact the deflowering of your teenage virgin?' She was going to cry any second now. She was going to break down and weep! 'Have the countless lovers who've passed through your bed not quite lived up to the excitement of having your very own personally trained sex object, one untouched by another male hand?'

'Well, I am sure the last part no longer counts,' he threw back in derision.

And how would you know? You haven't even bothered to ask how I was doing in five years! Louisa wanted to shout. Instead she took off down the track again, hating him so much she just couldn't understand how he could still get to her the way that he did!

Her knees still felt as if they didn't want to support her. Her body was on fire. Her angry eyes flashed forked lightning out into the darkness in front of her and her pulsing mouth shook with tears.

She caught her toe on another stone jutting up in the pathway—the same toe she'd hit before! As she stumbled with the same sound issuing forth from her throat a curse rattled out from behind her as an arm looped around her in a flying hook that launched her off the ground. The next few seconds went by in a grappling blur as a pair of running shoes fought for friction on the loose gravel slope. She was winded yet sobbing and panting at the same time.

Setting her feet down on the path, Andreas spun her round to face the full fury her reckless dash had unleashed. 'Are you crazy or something?' he bit down at her. 'How many fatal falls in this family will it take to make you—?'

He stopped like a man who'd been frozen. A white ring of tension circled the tense shape of his mouth. He wasn't looking at her. He wasn't looking at anything. And his fingers bit like talons into her arms while the night air screamed out what he had not said.

He'd meant Nikos. He'd been referring to the fatal fall their son had taken on a path just like this.

'Oh, dear God,' Louisa choked, how could she have been so stupidly thoughtless? 'I just didn't think,' she whispered painfully.

He suddenly came alive with a hard, tight, rasping rip of the air from his body. Before she knew what was happening he'd heaved her upwards until their faces were level and caught her quivering mouth with the all-consuming delivery of his. Half a second later and true pandemonium broke out, the passion of before swung back into dominance with a hot and seething sexual urgency that grabbed hold tight.

Louisa didn't even know which of them was first to fall victim. All she did recall was her head jerking back so she could look into his burning black eyes and any hint of common sense or self-control was tossed aside as their mouths met again in a wide, tight compulsion that she fell into mindlessly.

So much for not wanting sex on a dusty pathway, she thought hazily as he pushed her down onto one of the grassy embankments that ran along both sides of the path. The kiss didn't even break as they made the manoeuvre, lips fused, tongues seducing, claiming—demanding. Louisa was the one to push up his T-shirt to expose his beautiful muscular body before her shirt followed suit.

He released a husky groan as her breasts arrived against his hot naked flesh. She went up in flames. Their hands were all over each other; nothing in the least bit sophisticated about this. It was sexual compulsion taken down to its most basic function. They devoured each other with touch and taste—aroused and tormented each other, the gasping tugs of their breathing twisting all around them, wanting, demanding and getting without question. When Andreas reared back to strip the white cotton trousers from her legs, Louisa stared at the hard contours of his face, strapped tight by a need that reverberated inside herself, then she dropped her gaze to the proud jut at his thighs she had already exposed and caressed with her hands to bring him to this virile state.

'You always were a witch,' he husked as he came back to her, and his thick curse was only part of what was attacking him as he entered her with a single sweet, driving thrust.

Her shuddering gasp of pleasure brought his mouth back to hers to devour the sound. He drove into her like a man trapped in a fever. If she didn't know better she could have convinced herself that he had not done this for years. He was hot, he was trembling, his kiss so deep it was all she could do to clutch at his shoulders as he drove the whole wild experience on. As she began to reach that blinding white pinnacle he wrapped his strong arms right around her to lift her even closer and increased his pace. The tight sting of orgasm hit and just kept on coming, owning, controlling, flaying them both with its ripples of pleasure that dragged him groaning into the same frantic place.

Reality hit later when it was over. An awful silence filling with the terrible knowledge of the way they had behaved. It hit them both with a cold wash of dismay followed by a bone-tensing question as to what they were going to do next to extricate themselves from this.

Andreas muttered an earthy expletive as a final shudder shook him in the act of attempting to withdraw. Something tugged him right back again and Louisa's thick little whimper confirmed what that something was. She had just come all round him in a wild multi-orgasmic flow yet she still wasn't ready to let him go.

Or her inner body wasn't, he amended that as he felt her clenched fists push at his chest. 'Get off,' she choked out.

He leapt backwards, ignoring the next protesting shudder to hit him as he shot to his feet and turned his back on her while he straightened his clothing and allowed her the privacy to do the same thing.

Turning his back had not been a good idea, he realised a few seconds later after watching the white trousers slide out of his line of vision and he listened to the urgent rustle of clothing as she got dressed.

Eventually everything went still. The new silence flicked like a whip all around him. How the hell did he turn and face her now? What was he supposed to say to the woman he had just tossed down on the ground and taken in an utterly primitive, no-finesse, raging lust?

His wife. The mother of his son…

He compromised by only half turning, his eyes carefully hidden beneath the heavy droop of his eyelids as he stretched out a hand in a silent offer to help her to her feet.

She ignored it and scrambled up under her own steam. Her hair and her clothes were speckled with dirt and bits of dry grass and thyme, and she was trembling so badly she almost stumbled again.

'I—'

'Don't.' Her voice shook as she silenced him.

Heaving in his breath, Andreas supposed that she was probably right and silence at this moment was the only way to deal with what they had just done. Yet right on the back of that grim thought a sudden thick laugh caught hold of him. 'We never could control it, could we?'

It was like lifting the lid off a volcano, she launched the flat of her palm at his face.

'No…' He caught her wrist before the hand had a chance to make contact. 'You don't slap my face because you cannot control yourself around me, Louisa.'

'I hate you,' she whispered, wrenching her wrist free so she could spin her back to him, her slender arms wrapping around her body in soul-cutting self-defence. 'How could we do that?' she tremored. 'How could we just fall on each other like that?'

'It never took much.' His voice was grim again.

She swung back. 'Is that any kind of excuse?'

Andreas just shrugged. He'd wanted her from the moment he had watched her walk off the ferry. And, even standing here regretting the whole damn mad incident, he felt fresh need already pumping away inside him like some greedy monster he had never been able to feed anywhere else.

He cast a glance at the way she was standing there, upset, shaking with shock and horror and the close onset of tears. Beautiful, he thought bleakly, still so beautiful, even with her hair all over the place and her clothes covered with dirt.

'Wh-what if I get pregnant again?'

It came out of nowhere, the one thing he had not been prepared to hear. It totally shook him. 'You said that to punish me,' he pushed out hoarsely.

The way those dark blue eyes looked at him gave him his answer long before the breathy little, 'No,' arrived in his ears.

He bit out a word that made her wince, her kiss-swollen mouth quivering before she shot back bitterly, 'Well, that just about covers it.'

Then she left him standing there. Throat clogged by hot, shamed tears, Louisa started walking. When he came up behind her, her shoulders racked up with rejection because she thought he was going to grab her again.

But he didn't grab. 'Just walk,' he rasped as he stepped in front of her then began to lead the way back down the path.

Louisa followed him in thick, bubbling silence, shame consuming her a little more with each step. She did not look at him but kept her eyes fixed on the ground as they trod the soft sand on the beach. When they arrived at the hotel he stopped at the entrance and she kept on going. Neither bothered to offer up a hypocritical 'goodnight'.

When she finally crawled back into bed she hid her head beneath the pillow and tossed bitter recriminations at herself until she finally dropped into an exhausted sleep only to be woken up a few hours later by a knock on her bedroom door.

Struggling to drag herself awake, she rolled out of the bed without knowing she had done it. Then her eyes connected with the pile of clothes left to fall where she'd dropped them and instant recall had her falling like a stone back onto the mattress as the whole shocking episode robbed her of the ability to stand up.

She'd had sex with Andreas like a slut with no morals. She cringed inside her own flesh.

'Louisa!' Jamie knocked again. 'Breakfast—I'm starving!'

'Coming,' she called weakly. 'S-see you down there.' Then she dived for the damning heap of clothes and stuffed them to the bottom of her bag with urgent, trembling fingers as if hiding the evidence would take the crime away.

It didn't. As she headed for the bathroom she groaned at the subtle aches in places that made her quiver in shame and she hated herself. Catching sight of her face in the mirror froze her to the spot in dismay. She looked washed out through lack of sleep and all tumbled and tousled. A shocking inner glow burned like a sultry secret in the darkened blue of her eyes and in the soft pulse of her still swollen mouth.

I look like a lush, she thought in disgust and spun away from the mirror to step beneath the punishing heat of the shower spray.

Ten minutes later, showered, dressed and feeling about as composed as she was ever going to feel, she joined her brother on the shady terrace that overlooked the beach. The sun was already hot and glinting like crystal on the blue water. As they sat quietly planning their day while they ate breakfast, vivid flashbacks of what she and Andreas had done kept catching her out to send her senses spinning into hot, dipping dives.

Someone stepped around the corner of the hotel building from the direction of the car park. Glancing up, she felt her senses take a different kind of dive.

Well, this is a first in five years, she thought cynically as her mother-in-law walked towards their table.

'Kalimera, Louisa,' Isabella Markonos greeted pleasantly. 'Jamie, *pethi mou,* how you have grown since I saw you last!'

Flushing, Jamie stood up to suffer the airbrush of lips to his cheeks then hurriedly excused himself. He'd managed to arrange a lift into town with Yannis's son Pietros which gave him a great excuse to escape.

'The years have flown by so fast,' Isabella murmured wistfully as she watched him beat his hasty retreat.

Louisa said absolutely nothing and after a short hesitation her mother-in-law took possession of Jamie's vacated seat then lifted dark eyes to her face.

'Andreas has left the island,' she informed her gently. 'He visited Nikos very early this morning then boarded his helicopter and flew away…'

CHAPTER FIVE

ANDREAS had gone...?

Louisa had to fight to hang on to a calm expression.

'He is very angry with me,' Isabella confided. 'And I can see from the look in your eyes that you are angry with me too.'

Was that what her look said? Better than looking devastated, she supposed. 'You had no right to interfere,' she said.

'When have I not interfered between the two of you?' the older woman hit back. 'Who else was there to do it? You were two children playing at being adults for most of your marriage. You needed someone to interfere simply to keep you both practical.'

Practical. Louisa almost let loose a laugh. When had she and Andreas ever been *practical* about this attraction they suffered for each other? Certainly not up there last night on the hill. And if Isabella wanted to go back that far, then who wanted to be practical at the age of seventeen or twenty-two?

Isabella had been very practical when she'd gently suggested that Louisa should have her pregnancy terminated. Louisa recalled the way she'd wept to Andreas, and he'd turned on his mother and hit the roof. Later, when Nikos was born, Isabella then gently suggested that she should take care of her grandson while Louisa finished her education—in England. Again she had wept and again Andreas had angrily turned on his mother.

'It was me who suggested you might prefer to visit Nikos when you could be sure that Andreas would not be here.' Isabella picked on the only practical suggestion she'd ever made that Louisa had no argument with. 'It was therefore down to me to make the decision that such a situation could not be allowed to go on.'

Sitting back in her seat, Louisa looked at this beautiful, dainty Greek woman who possessed a heart of steel behind all the visible signs of softer living, and wondered what her practical solution was going to be if her son had to break the news to her that he could have made his estranged wife pregnant again?

'You both need to move on with your lives,' Isabella continued, unaware of what was going on inside Louisa's head. 'It has become very clear to me that neither of you were going to do that until you had confronted your past.'

'So you set Andreas and me up for a face-to-face confrontation?'

'You needed to look at each other and *see* that you are no longer the same two people you used to be—see for yourselves how widely you have grown apart!'

A vibrant flashback in which she'd played a very intimate part in Andreas's life recently hit Louisa's vision.

'We came to love you dearly, Louisa,' Isabella persisted in her oh-so-deceptive gentle voice. 'And we hurt deeply for both you and my son when fate dealt you such a cruel tragic blow. My dearest wish would be to see both of you happy again—in love and married to some other wonderful person who will give you more children to help heal the gap in your hearts dear Nikos left behind.'

In a sad, painfully aching way, Louisa agreed with those wishes. She too would like to be truly happy again. But how could she ever be happy with someone else when the man she had been in love with since she was seventeen still commanded so much power over her?

'It is time for you both to let go…'

It was the way Isabella said it that grabbed Louisa's full attention. 'You want me to stop coming to the island,' she said.

For a moment Isabella said nothing, allowing her answer to sound in the paining silence that hovered over them for a second or two. Then she stood up and came round the table. As she bent to kiss Louisa's cheek she repeated gently, 'It is time.'

Then she walked away, leaving Louisa on her own to absorb that cold little stab of cruel truth.

Andreas had already left the island, making his statement about letting go by putting distance between them as quickly as he could. His mother was now telling her that when she left here she would prefer it if she did not come back.

She got up, tense—shivery suddenly though the sun was hot. Andreas had gone. His mother did not want her here. Up on the hill above the harbour stood a tiny domed chapel with its neatly kept gardens where her son had been laid to rest. Did Nikos need her to come here? Did she have to come all this way to find him? He lived in her heart, would always live there, she knew that, but—

The *but* suddenly lost itself in the next thought to shoot into her head. She had done a very stupid thing last night and now retribution was looming large in the form of a pregnancy she could not allow to become real.

Truly pale now, the natural creamy tone of her skin wiped away, Louisa moved across the terrace like someone not of this life. An hour later and she was in town, standing outside the old-fashioned pharmacy with its distinctive green and white sign above the door. Tears were in her eyes and one of her hands was covering her trembling mouth because she knew now that she couldn't do it. She just could not walk in there and calmly ask for the morning-after pill as if the tiny thing maybe struggling for life inside her did not have rights of its own.

It would be a part of her, a part of Andreas—a special part of their son. How she had even been able to convince herself she could just take a pill to ensure no child would come from what had taken place last night was appalling her now.

Let nature make the decision, she told herself as she turned and walked away again. Surely fate would not be so cruel as to make her pregnant again. Didn't they say that lightning never struck in the same place twice?

She spent the next few days almost entirely with Jamie. She was quiet and withdrawn, though he was too busy enjoying himself to notice. Each morning they would eat breakfast together then he would walk her up to the chapel on the hill, stay with her for a little while before shooting off again, leaving her alone while he went back to the hotel.

Reclining on a sun bed in the shade of an umbrella, Louisa spent the rest of her day watching as Pietros, the hotel owner's son, showed Jamie how to windsurf or how to ride his pride-and-joy jet ski, and they even talked someone into taking them out on his speedboat so that Jamie could try his hand at water-skiing too.

She tried *not* to think about Andreas. She tried *not* to beat herself up over what they had done. She tried not to agonise over the decision she had made outside the pharmacy. It won't come to anything, she kept telling herself.

Then there were other times when Isabella's blunt speaking would suddenly grab hold of her and she would take off on a tight-limbed, restless walk down the beach and battle with the tumbling morass of other feelings that swirled around her. It was a battle because, deep down, Lousia knew that Isabella was right. She had to let this island go.

Let Nikos go.

Let his father go.

Dressed in a pale blue wrap-around skirt and white summer top, Louisa sat on the stone seat set beside her son's little grave with its marble headstone gleaming white in the sun. Today marked the fifth anniversary of his passing and she was glad she'd been able to convince Jamie to go with Pietros on a boat that was going out fishing for the day.

She needed to be on her own.

Moving to rest her forearms along the length of her sun-warmed thighs, she looked around her through blue eyes misted by the love she felt for this place. There was nowhere more beautiful on this earth than this tiny corner of Greece in her opinion. All around her the loving care and attention laboured on each square inch of the chapel and its garden was there to see in the carefully tended graves and the profusion of colour bursting from flowers that bloomed hot and bright in the fierce summer heat. Birds sang. The air was full of the scent of summer jasmine, and the tiny chapel with its handsome dome stood backed by a clear blue sky.

Nikos had been baptised here. She and Andreas had been married here, watched by curious islanders. She had been the quintessentially shy and uncertain blushing bride but because she had been carrying Andreas's baby she had felt as if everyone looked on her as if—

Curtailing that memory, because it did not really matter any more what other people had once thought about her, she tried to concentrate on the here and now, and another painful decision she still had to make.

Did she leave here on the ferry in a few days' time and never come back?

Lowering her face to her hands, she let her silk blonde hair flood forward to hide her face. It was all so muddled up, so painful and complicated. She wanted to think only about Nikos but all she could think about was herself! What was happening to her? What was going on inside her head?

A shadow suddenly fell across the sun to douse her in shadow. Pulling her face out of her hands, she had to squint to take in the tall, dark silhouette standing there. She couldn't see his face because the sun was coming from directly behind him but she knew who it was.

'When did you get back?' she questioned flatly.

'This morning,' he said. 'I had to leave quickly because of some business I could not neglect but...'

He shifted his stance, leaving the rest of his sentence unfinished as if he wished he had not said it at all. And the way he shoved his hands into the pockets of his trousers told her that he wasn't comfortable here.

Or he was uncomfortable about being here with her, Louisa amended and sent her gaze drifting towards something sitting on the white marble ledge of their son's headstone that had not been there the day before, which told her Andreas had been here once already today.

Early.

So as to avoid bumping into her.

Even after five long years, did he still find it this difficult to be here with her?

'We need to talk.'

'Not today, Andreas,' she refused quietly.

'My mother told me what she said to you. She—'

Damn interfering Isabella. 'You've bought a new car,' she cut in.

'I don't want you to listen to her. She—'

'Another Ferrari,' she interrupted. 'A black one instead of your favourite red.'

'It is no one else's business what you or I—'

'Do you think you're too old for flashy red now, is that it?'

Reaching forward, she plucked up the little black toy Ferrari from its narrow shelf with a dry little smile softening her unhappy face. Each time she'd come here over the years, the little car had been changed for a different model. It was one of those small things that always touched a tender spot inside her because she knew it was Andreas who brought them here and that it usually meant he had also changed one of his many super-cars he had scattered around the globe.

'I just felt like a change, that's all,' he answered gruffly, then impatiently, 'Will you listen to me, Louisa? We need—'

'You big liar, Andreas Markonos,' she said. 'You decided that red Ferraris are for the flashy young-bloods and you've grown much too sophisticated to be one of them so you bought black this time. Nikos is going to be so—'

'Will you not speak like that!' he ground out.

Louisa's whole body jolted in shock at his anger. 'Like what?' she quavered.

He swung his back to her, swivelling on the heels of his black leather shoes. 'As if he is still alive.'

Trembling now, all hint of softness wiped clean, Louisa replaced the little car on its ledge. Tension sawed into the thickening silence. Pushing her hands flat together in front of her, she said nothing. In a tangled sort of way, she understood. She did speak of Nikos as if he were still right here with her. Sometimes the feeling was so strong she could actually believe he was...

Pulling in a thick breath, she stood up as that sudden restlessness grabbed hold of her again to send her walking across the soft green of the carefully watered lawn to end up standing against the low wall that enclosed the chapel grounds, feeling as if the letting-go stuff was beginning to crowd in on her from all sides.

After a few seconds Andreas followed, making the fine hairs at the back of her neck tingle when he came to a stop behind her. 'My apologies,' he said heavily. 'I did not intend to shout at you like that.'

Louisa dismissed his need to apologise with a tense little shrug. Her restlessness had nothing to do with his emotional outburst. This was after all a very emotive place.

Feeling the corner of her mouth tug down on a sad little grimace, 'Do you come here a lot?' she asked him quietly.

'Each time I visit the island,' he responded.

Louisa nodded. 'But you belong here.'

No reply came to that. He *did* belong here. Whereas she did not.

Staring out towards the expanse of glistening blue ocean until her eyes began to sting, 'This is the last time I will be coming here,' she told him, voicing the decision she had been struggling with for days.

'Don't be foolish!' he snapped. 'As I have been trying to say to you, you don't have to heed my mother's interference!'

'She's right though. It is time I let go.'

'Time,' he repeated as if it were a rude word. 'What has time got to do with what we leave behind here each time we have to go away?'

'You feel that too?' Swinging round to face him, Louisa released a sharp gasp when she found herself looking at a completely different man from the one she had expected to see.

Until now she had only seen him wrapped in the softening cloak of darkness and he had been too dangerously potent for her to deal with then. Looking into his lean face without the sun blinding her eyes, she now felt the impact of this new view of him with a shattering shock. The younger man she had first fallen in love with had gone—forever. What she'd seen as mere maturity under cover of darkness had done him absolutely no justice at all. He was totally, devastatingly handsome. Totally, devastatingly lean—both physically and on the inside, where it only showed in the aura she was picking up from him. Andreas was a man to whom compromise had become very thinly spread indeed. The mouth that had kissed her so thoroughly a few nights ago now had a hardness about it that placed a chill across her bones. And the eyes, those deep-set dark brown eyes, looked as though the darker passions of the other night were as alien to him as—as standing here in this pretty place talking with her at all!

'Of course I feel it,' he said harshly. 'Do you think I am made of stone?'

'Yes!' Louisa heard herself answer. But worse than that, she was finally—finally feeling the full blunt impact of what his mother had been talking about. She was finally seeing *why* Isabella wanted the two of them to come face to face. The ordinary English girl and this powerful Greek man were in such different leagues now that if they'd met for the first time this week Andreas would not have given her a second glance!

Her arms wrapped tightly around her middle. She dragged her eyes away from him—but not before they'd taken in the sharply tailored dark business suit in some expensive fabric that made such a big statement about his wealth and how comfortable he was with the stunning sophistication with which he wore it. Even the way his pale blue shirt collar sat so smoothly around his brown throat made its own statement about an exclusivity he had been gifted with from birth. Seeing it all set Louisa reeling because—how was it that she hadn't noticed this staggeringly elegant man developing inside him while they'd still been together as man and wife?

'How can you even be considering deserting our son?' he rasped at her.

Having to force herself to concentrate on what he'd just said to her, Louisa tugged some air into her lungs. 'Haven't you just told me that he isn't here?' she reminded him. 'And you're right,' she added when his dark eyes flicked like hard black diamonds and his tense mouth parted to say something. 'Nikos left here a long time ago. Travelling all the way out here once a year to visit what is really only a shrine to him is a pretty meaningless exercise when I know exactly where I can find him when I need him.'

'Look at *me* when you say that,' Andreas responded tautly. 'Look into my face and tell me again that this place, this island, that small grave over there no longer mean a thing to you!'

The force of his anger widened her eyes on him. 'That was not what I said,' she denied. 'And why are you so angry with me?' she demanded. 'Until a few days ago you were not even aware that I came here at all!'

His body tensed inside all of that elegant dark suiting. 'That has nothing to do with it.'

'Well, thanks,' Louisa murmured bitterly.

Something ripped across his hard features. 'I mean that we are not discussing my failings here, we—'

'So you do know you have them.'

He twisted away from her but even the way he did that was smoothly controlled and elegantly graceful instead of packed full with those old unfettered passions belonging to the younger man she had once known—the man she had met on a hill the other night!

'As soon as you could after we buried Nikos you walked away from me,' she reminded him bleakly.

The chiselled edge of his jaw flexed. 'There were too many people around. I—needed to be alone.'

'And I didn't?'

'I am a man. It's OK for a woman to break down and

weep in front of others but a man must remain strong and supportive.'

Louisa uttered a thick laugh. 'Well, you certainly failed there, Andreas.'

His hands came out of his pockets and bunched into fists and she knew they did. She'd hit a nerve and the sadness of it all was that she just did not care. He'd hurt her badly when he'd walked away from her that day and even now, five years on, she still found it impossible to forgive him for doing that.

They'd had a fight via the telephone the day that Nikos had taken his fatal fall. Andreas had been telling her that he had to stay in Athens to attend an important board meeting. He'd insisted that he had no choice. She'd insisted that everyone had choices and that it was his choice to break his promise to spend the day on the beach with his son! Then she'd slammed down the phone and made her choice to take Nikos to the beach by herself.

As she lowered her head, her eyes turned dark like a bottomless ocean as she relived the moment that Nikos had broken free of her grasp and begun to run down the dusty track towards a herd of goats. She could still hear the way she had called out to him, 'Nikos, take care!' and still see the way one of the goats leapt from the embankment to land directly in his path.

'You left because you blamed me for what happened,' she whispered.

He spun around, a shaft of hard shock on his face. 'I did not!'

Still, Louisa sent him a look of bleak disbelief. Why wouldn't he blame her when she blamed herself?

'I did not blame you.' He grabbed her arm when she went to spin away from him. 'It was an accident. Apportioning blame to such a tragedy is a weak fool's way of dealing with it.'

Which was all very wise and grown-up, Louisa thought with a rueful twist of her mouth, but five years ago they had been neither wise nor grown-up, had they?

'Where did you go when you left here?' she questioned after yet another taut moment scrambled between them.

Letting go of her arm, he released a sigh. 'I flew to the apartment in Athens and just stayed there. By the time I returned here to the island you had already left with your family.'

'Two weeks later, Andreas,' Louisa provided. 'I waited two weeks for you to come back.'

His dark eyes were steady on her, not a hint of apology in them. 'And you, *agape mou*, gave me only two weeks to come to my senses before deciding to go…'

It was the cool counter-challenge, Louisa recognised. It was the new tougher male with compromise spread very thin. She could have said more. She could have reminded him how he had not called her once while she'd been in England to ask how she was coping. She could even explain how she'd come back to the island six miserable weeks later, only to discover that he was not here. Or she could tell him how she'd flown to Athens and gone to their apartment, witnessed for herself what he had been doing to blot her out of his life.

But why bother when all of that was in the past and the consensus of opinion was that it was time to let the past go? It was over between them. It had been over for the last five years, which only made the lusty romp on the hill all the more shameful and what might come from it something she could repent at her leisure once she got back home.

Taking a blind glance at her watch, 'I'm supposed to be meeting Jamie in ten minutes,' she lied and walked away from him.

CHAPTER SIX

ANDREAS watched her go with his eyes narrowed and his chest feeling as if it was about to explode.

Blame her? He was still struggling to believe she had actually said that. How could she possibly think that he would blame her for anything when it had to be patently obvious that the only person he'd ever blamed for what had happened was himself?

Swinging away, he glared at the ocean. He should have been there. He should have been keeping his promise to his wife and his son instead of playing the big tycoon who found the alluring drug of power more important to him than them.

Well, he'd learnt that lesson in life the hardest way. She had accepted none of his calls to her parents' house while she'd been in England. She'd switched off her mobile phone. When he'd flown to London to see her he'd been stonewalled by her cold-faced parents telling him that their daughter did not want to see him or speak to him. After that kick in the gut he'd flown back to Athens and spent the next few weeks stone-cold drunk.

Turning round, he saw she was in the process of squatting down and kissing her fingertips before gently pressing them to their son's bright white marble headstone. His throat tightened, a whole gamut of aches raking through him as he watched her remain there like that with the hot sun beating down on her golden head and her fingers lingering where she had placed them.

So what next? he mused grimly. Where did the two of them go from here?

Not where that cold little look she'd sent him before she walked away said they were going anyway, he determined. This was not over yet by a long way and the sooner Louisa came to terms with that, the easier it was going to be for both of them.

By the time Louisa straightened up he was at her side again. 'I will drive you back to the hotel.'

'I can walk,' she refused.

There was a short pause followed by one of those impatient shifts of his body, then his voice arrived so close to her ear it wove words around her like silk. 'Perhaps I should tell you that Father Lukas is standing by the chapel entrance watching us,' he murmured. 'Do you want to give him fresh gossip to spread about us while we have yet another argument right here across our son's grave?'

It was the 'our son's grave' part that reached her, the sheer irreverence of arguing here at all. Taking a quick glance from beneath the shelter of her eyelashes to check that what he was saying about the priest was true, 'OK,' she conceded grudgingly. 'I will accept the lift.'

'Thank you,' he drawled drily, then made her muscles stiffen as one of his hands slipped around her slender waist as he bent across her and reached out with his other hand to straighten the already perfectly straight little toy car on its ledge.

The warm, tangy scent of him swirled around her senses, the hot sun picked out the blackness of his hair and the rich golden colour of his skin. She tried to relax in his light grasp, tried not to notice the way his fingers lingered on the white marble ledge for a few more seconds before he slid them away and straightened up again. But the sudden sting gathering in her eyes and her throat was the sting of thick tears because she knew that his lingering touch on the toy car meant the same to a Greek male who did not show his emotions in public as the tender farewell kiss she'd just pressed to the marble stone.

'Let's go,' he said gruffly and turned her towards the gap in the wall which led to the car park.

'W-we should go and speak to Father Lukas,' she managed to mumble across the threatening tears.

'He will not want to intrude on our privacy today of all days,' Andreas said quietly. 'Unless, of course,' he then added smoothly, 'you want me to ask him how quickly he can arrange the renewal of our marriage vows.'

That totally unexpected, truly sardonic comment sent Louisa lurching from hot tears into a bristling fury she had to fight to keep down if she didn't want Father Lukas to see her blow up.

'I'm going to pretend that you never said that,' she whispered hotly. 'That way you won't get blood on your fancy suit!'

'I take it that renewing our vows is not to your liking, then?' Andreas responded lightly.

'Being near you at all is not to my liking!' Louisa flung back.

'Shame you did not think about that the other night.'

Louisa gave up trying to behave and went to wrench free of him. 'I don't know where you get the flat arrogance to believe you can joke about it!'

'No joke.' Long fingers pinned her right where she was.

'Well, you're mad, then, if you're daring to think I actually *want* to stay married to you!'

'Well, no child of mine will be born out of wedlock,' he informed her. 'So divorce is out, which leaves us with—what option left?'

Divorce…?

With that one casually uttered word he shattered her. It was like driving at full speed into a brick wall. For all the long hours she'd battled with *letting go* of their past, the crazily logical solution of divorce had not so much as entered her head!

Why hadn't it?

She pulled to a shuddering stop in the dusty car park. *Divorce*, she repeated to herself. The final solution. It was sensible. It brought proper closure to everything—freed them both to get on with the rest of their lives.

So why was she feeling as if she was being turned inside out?

Andreas twisted to stand in front of her, his hands coming to rest on her shoulders, his voice a low, husky rasp. 'Stop trembling,' he muttered. 'It isn't as if we…' He ground to a stop suddenly, the black bars of his eyebrows pulling together across the bridge of his nose as his fingers lightly tested the heat in her skin. 'How long have you been sitting out here in the sun?' he demanded.

Dusky eyelashes flickering away from turbulent blue eyes, she barely heard what he had said. 'I'm not pregnant,' she whispered.

'I thought you had more sense than to sit in the sun without shelter,' he muttered. 'Now your lovely skin is so hot it—'

'Andreas— I am *not* pregnant!' she choked out.

His fingers stilled on her burning shoulders, a muscle twitched at the corner of his mouth. He looked into her eyes, her wide, blue, anxious eyes. 'But you are seriously concerned that you could be,' he said, 'or you would not have spent several minutes standing outside the pharmacy the other morning fighting with yourself before deciding that you could not do it.'

It was just one hard shock too many. The breath came and went from her body in appalled understanding of what that coolly delivered statement actually meant. 'You've been having me watched!'

He didn't even bother to deny it, just clasped her arm and led her across the last few metres to where his car was parked then leant past her to open the door.

'Get in,' was all he said.

When she turned to argue with him a cold chill went chasing through her because he looked so stern, so unrelentingly *tough*, and on a sudden bright flash of understanding it hit her that during his days away from the island Andreas had come to some serious decisions about them.

'Why?' she whispered shakily.

Irritation flicked across his hard-boned features. 'Because I am not indulging in a stand-up fight with you here?'

His sarcasm hissed the air from her body. 'Don't be so—'

He pulled her against him then lowered his head and captured her mouth. It wasn't an angry kiss or even a passionate kiss, it was a—frustrated, compulsive, shut-up kind of kiss that locked the two of them together in a dusty car park with the sun beating relentlessly down on their heads.

'That,' he husked out as he drew away again, 'was for Father Lukas. Now get in the damn car before I take the next one for myself!'

Shaken—shocked some more because she'd forgotten all about the watchful priest standing in the church doorway, Louisa subsided into the low car seat. She pretended not to notice the way Andreas dropped his glinting gaze to her legs as the wrap-around skirt slithered open to reveal the length of a long and slender thigh, pale as porcelain and as smooth as silk—before her trembling fingers covered it up.

He closed the car door with a sharp flick from long fingers then strode around the bonnet with her wide blue eyes fixed on his tall, lean bulk as it moved with a smooth animal grace. His dark suit shifted expensively against him as he opened the other door then got in beside her, making her mouth go dry, because once again she was recognising that this Andreas was a completely different kind of beast from the one she had used to know.

'Why have me watched?' she demanded as he stretched out a hand to turn the key in the ignition.

The engine fired. He slipped it into gear. 'I had to go back to Athens for a few days,' he answered. 'We had just enjoyed unprotected sex and I could not be sure what you would do about it once the shock had worn off, so I had one of my security team flown in to keep an eye on you.'

His security team? Her image of him was growing bigger and bigger. 'For what purpose?' she snapped out. 'To stop me from throwing myself off the peninsula in despair—or to push me off it if I went near the edge?'

'I protect my own,' was all he said, as if that should mean something to her.

Well, it didn't. 'I do not belong to you.'

The square cut of his chin jutted as he turned them around in the car park. 'As my wife you belong to me, as does the child in your womb.'

'If there is one—*if*!'

Car tyres crunched as they drove over gravel. A few seconds later they were turning onto the road. 'You had your chance to make it a definite no, Louisa, and decided not to take it.'

Heat flooded her cheeks. 'I will not apologise for that decision.'

'Did I ask you to?' He sent her a cool glance as the car accelerated away, all slick, smooth man of the minute, she observed with a resentful sting. A sophisticated man in his sophisticated suit driving his sophisticated car, wearing a sophisticatedly implacable expression on his too, too handsome face.

'Implied it,' she said, seeing herself sitting beside him in her high-street skirt and little top and with about as much sophistication running in her blood to make a complete mockery of the fact that they had ever been drawn to each other in the first place!

'Then I apologise. It was not intentional.'

'How did your henchman know what I was thinking outside the pharmacy anyway?' she flung out.

'He didn't. He merely relayed your movements to me and I drew my own conclusions.'

'So you're very clued up on tacky things like the morning-after pill?'

'As, by all accounts, are you,' he returned. 'In truth,' he added after a moment, 'at first I thought you must be hovering over going in the shop to buy a pregnancy-testing kit. It only occurred to me later that you could only be so upset if you had been considering the—other thing.'

Louisa froze where she sat, she was so stunned that she had not thought of buying the test kit herself!

Twisting round in her seat, 'Take me into town and I will buy a test right now,' she said urgently.

'And give the islanders something to really gossip about?'

He had an answer to everything. Sinking back in the seat she seethed in silence for a few seconds—then suddenly took notice of where they were.

'You've gone the wrong way—the hotel is in the other direction.'

His answer was a quick, smooth change through the gears and an indifferent profile.

'Andreas…'

'I know where we are going,' he drawled.

'But,' not liking this, not liking the tight, tingling feeling that was telling her she had lost control of everything that was happening here, 'I need to go back to the hotel,' she insisted. 'I'm meeting Jamie there in less than five minutes and you—'

'Liar,' he said. 'I met Jamie in town this morning. He has gone fishing for the day with Yannis's son.'

Silence met that. Andreas turned his head to study the way she was sitting there with her silky blonde hair blowing back from the delicate formation of her face so she could not hide the guilty look at being caught out with the lie. She was not breathing as far as he could see and her teeth were pressing sharp crescents into her soft lower lip.

'He did the protective-brother thing and warned me to stay away from you,' he extended coolly.

'Oh, he didn't.' She closed her eyes on a groan.

Turning his attention back to the road, 'It was his right to do it,' Andreas shrugged. 'I respect him for it.'

'What did you say to him?'

'I told him nicely to stay out of it,' he responded. 'Then I loaned him some money because he was hovering around the bank, which was closed, and the wall machine was not working.'

'Jamie accepted a loan—from *you*?'

Her disbelief made him grimace. 'Not without a bit of manly posturing,' he admitted. 'Then, because he did not like to take anything from me without some pay-back, he told me about an enterprising guy called Max Landreau…'

The air inside the open-top car had been circulating quite pleasantly but at that precise moment it seemed to go perfectly still. Lifting up her chin and turning her face to the sun-kissed coastline speeding by her side of the car, Louisa pressed her lips together and refused to say a single word.

Tension inched into the sun-drenched vehicle.

'Who is he?' Andreas asked when it became clear she was going to say nothing at all.

Building an image of Max's tall dark shape in her head, she paused before answering, 'That is none of your business.'

The hiss of his breath kept her chin up and her face averted. 'He could become my business if you slept with him before you came here.'

That twisted her head around. 'I beg your pardon?' she prompted indignantly.

'If you are pregnant,' he enlightened, 'we could have a paternity question to deal with. Very messy.'

'And who have *you* slept with in the last month?' she flicked back.

He frowned. 'My recent sex life could not become a problem.'

'If you were as careless with her as you were with me it could be! Now, there's an interesting concept,' Louisa laughed through her shimmering anger. 'Two of your sexual partners pregnant at the same time…What will you do in your quest to have no child of yours born out of wedlock, Andreas? Dump the wife and marry the mistress?'

'We were discussing your relationship with Landreau.' He frowned. 'Jamie said the guy wants to marry you.'

'Well, lucky me,' she mocked, thinking—you wretch, Jamie! 'So which do *I* choose; the useless husband or the fabulous lover?'

Long fingers flexed on the steering wheel at her very measured insult aimed at his sexual prowess. 'I am being serious.'

'Well, I am seriously *not* going to be pregnant,' Louisa flashed. 'And if I am unlucky enough to find out that I have conceived a baby I will *not* play the role of your unworthy wife again!'

'Tell our son that.'

The pained gasp she released hurt her throat and brought his face swinging round to flick a hard crushing look. Angry did not cover it, uncompromising ruthlessness did.

'Tell Nikos that you are not prepared to sacrifice everything for his brother or sister in the same way that you did for him.'

'Now who's talking about him as if he's still with us?' Louisa pushed out chokily. 'And you should be ashamed of yourself for saying any of that at all!'

Breathing gone thickly haywire now, she turned her face away again, vibrating inside with hurt. Another silence stung between them like killer bees on the rampage. They'd almost reached the far end of the island when he swung the car off the road to dip down a track through a thicket of trees.

They came to a stop in a dusty clearing. The engine died. The mood between them was thick. Louisa was fighting the lumps of tears lodged in her throat. Andreas climbed out of the car and came round to her side. When he opened the door for her she just remained sitting there refusing to look at him, refusing to move. The arm that lanced across her to unfasten her seat belt brushed against her cheek and sent her head jolting backwards. The air hissed from between his clenched teeth in response because it was so clear that her reaction had been one of revulsion.

'I want to go back,' she insisted.

'Tough,' he roughed out, hard fingers closing around her wrist like a manacle so he could use it as a lever to haul her out of the car.

The fact that a slender white leg appeared through the

sliding gap in her skirt again did not improve his temper at all. She saw his face darken, saw the muscle-flexing clench of his gleaming white teeth. In its own way it was fascinating to watch him lose control of his temper like this. Like the old Andreas. Like the hotly jealous and possessive younger man who'd spent six weeks keeping her well away from his lusty Greek friends.

'You're hurting my wrist,' she protested.

Squared chin jutting, he turned and began pulling her towards a wide, squat building she had not noticed as they'd driven up. He did not loosen his grip.

'And bullies are not in the least bit attractive,' she added tightly.

'Shut up.' He came to a stop in front of a blue-painted door.

The building looked new, Louisa saw, trying hard to curb her curiosity as he twisted a key in the lock. The land surrounding the house was still half a building site and there was a mini-digger resting idle over by the trees.

It was all she had time to notice before she was being pulled inside. Only after he'd slammed the door firmly shut behind her did he release her wrist, then he strode off through a wide archway and down some steps, leaving her standing there staring at the angry set of his wide shoulders that shouted Arrogant Greek Male so loudly she wanted to throw something at him!

But she didn't have anything to throw and anyway she would *not* lower herself to his bullish level, she told herself as she rubbed at her wrist while glancing around. She discovered she was standing in a spacious hallway with rooms leading off from either side of the arch. The sense of newness was all around her in the smell of drying plaster and freshly applied paint on the walls and the clear fact that furniture of any description was scarce.

It struck her that she could just turn and open the door and walk away now that he'd left her standing here, and she even twisted in that direction, only to change her mind when she remembered it was at least a four-mile walk back to the hotel and it was hot out there and deliciously cool in here.

Anyway, curiosity was getting the better of her. What was this place?

With no intention of trailing in Andreas's footsteps to ask him, Louisa struck out in another direction, opening doors along the lobby and peering inside. Most of them seemed to be bedrooms. Some of them were furnished and others were completely bare. After she'd checked all the doors she stepped up to the central archway and found herself looking down on a huge white space with wall-to-wall windows at one end framing what looked from here like a fabulous ocean view. A couple of big sofas still wrapped in plastic occupied the centre of the floor and what looked like a large flat-screen television covered in bubble-wrap was fixed to one wall.

The whole place had an unfinished, unlived-in echo about it, she thought as she walked down the three shallow steps which took her into the room itself, the main sounds she could hear coming from beyond another archway cut into a side-wall.

It was a kitchen, she discovered as she stepped into the opening, a huge, glossy white kitchen with a wooden table standing in the middle of its white-tiled floor. It was all very new, very modern, with another wall of glass Andreas was in the process of sliding open to let in the breeze coming off the ocean.

He had removed his jacket and tossed it onto the table. Unwanted butterflies attacked low in her stomach as she slid her eyes over the pale blue shirting covering his long torso, then his narrow hips and legs, which seemed to have gained in length and pure, potent power with the jacket gone.

'What is this place?' she finally gave in and asked him.

'Mine.' He said it with a low, rasping economy that told her his mood had not improved at all.

So much for curiosity, she thought with a grimace, spied a huge fridge opposite and was drawn to it by a sudden raging thirst. Tugging open the doors, she discovered it had been stocked full with just about everything to tempt anyone's appetite. Ignoring the sudden hungry snap her stomach sent her, she selected a bottle of chilled water and unscrewed the cap as she elbowed the fridge doors shut.

Too thirsty to wait to hunt down a glass, she tipped back her head and drank greedily straight from the bottle. When she finally felt quenched enough to lower the bottle again, her blue eyes widened then stilled when she found that Andreas had turned and was staring through heavily hooded, glinting dark eyes at her extended throat.

Her heart gave a thump and a trickle of cool water lodged in her throat. She had to cough to clear it. The choky little sound brought his gaze up to lock onto the dews of water still clinging to her lips. Her very flesh began to tingle with that tight sting of overwhelming intimacy that came with the deeply bedded knowledge of everything about each other, which exposed what they were thinking or feeling even if neither wished to be so transparent. In this case Louisa would not have been in the least bit surprised if he'd leapt on her like a big hungry cat.

Because they'd always had this…gift for making the air between them pulse with sexual awareness. It had happened at the ferry terminal. It had happened on the hill. It had happened twice already today when he'd watched her wrap-around skirt slide apart. Andreas had looked at her exposed thigh and the heat of his desire to reach down and stroke her exposed flesh had struck right at the very centre of her sexual heart. Now here it was happening again as he stared at her water-dewed lips.

She licked the dew away with a flick of her tongue. The heavy black curves of his eyelashes flickered and the sizzling sting arrowed itself in a three-pronged attack on the tips of her breasts and between her thighs.

'Thirsty,' she said jerkily in the hope that speech would banish the unwanted sensation.

It didn't.

'How long had you been at the chapel before I arrived there?' he demanded huskily.

The husky tone didn't do much for her comfort either. 'I can't see that it matters.' She shrugged the question away while wishing to hell that he didn't look as good as he did.

'It matters if you have been foolish enough to let yourself become dehydrated.'

He was right, she was forced to acknowledge with a frown. She had desperately needed the water but now that its deliciously cooling effect had reached her stomach she was beginning to feel ever so slightly queasy, and the skin on her arms and her shoulders felt tight and hot, which told her she had spent way too long in the sun.

'Such husbandly concern,' she mocked, lifting the bottle up so she could read the label, just in case she'd accidentally drunk something more lethal that water, 'but it's absolutely wasted on me, Andreas, when I don't answer to you any more.'

'If I gathered you up and stretched you out on that table you would answer to me,' he growled out. 'So stop trying to pretend you don't give a damn about me when you know you still light up like a blowtorch whenever you look at me or I look at you.'

Stung by the horrible truth in that, 'Maybe I light up the same for any man,' Louisa retaliated. 'I mean, think of all those years I've had to manage without you around to light my torch!'

Taking him on in the mood he was in was pretty stupid, Louisa recognised the moment he took his hands out of his pockets and she saw the darkening look hardening his face.

'Well, that brings us neatly back to Max Landreau,' he said and began moving towards her, coming in so close it was all she could do not to take a defensive step back. But that would give him an edge she refused to let him have, so she held her ground even though that ground felt oddly shaky beneath her feet.

'I'm not going to talk to you about Max,' she declared stubbornly, then frowned when she realised that a lot of things felt rather shaky right now, including her voice.

Twisting the cap back on the bottle, she turned to place it on the counter and almost staggered when the quick movement made her head start to swim.

'Why not?'

Turning back to him, she frowned even more when his lean, dark bulk kept floating in and out of focus and nausea made a second grab at her stomach.

'I need the loo,' she said, fixing her muzzy gaze on the archway.

His hand closing around her arm stopped her from moving towards it. 'We will finish this before you walk away.'

'There is nothing to finish.' Tugging free of his grip, she stepped around him and tried her best to walk in a straight line, only to find Andreas had moved to block her path.

Staring dizzily at the dark blue strip of his tie hanging down the front of his shirt, she laid a hand across her churning stomach. 'Andreas, I don't…'

'You either tell me about Landreau or we do it the hard way,' he warned her grimly. 'And heed this, Louisa,' he added, 'you will not be leaving this house until I know everything about you and him—understand?'

Oh, she understood all right. Trying to ignore what was rumbling round inside her, she lifted her eyes to his angry face. 'Where do you get off believing that you have that right?'

He sucked in his breath. 'You are my wife. You belong to *me*.'

'I do not belong to *you*!' she cried out. 'Will you stop saying that? I stopped belonging to *you* when you didn't bother to come and get me five years ago! Now, please let me—'

'What do you mean, I didn't bother to come and get you? Where do *you* get off, telling a damn lie like that?'

This wasn't the time for this. She was in real danger of losing the contents of her stomach on his shoes if she didn't get to a loo quickly. But there was something in his harsh rasp that made her pause.

'You couldn't even manage a single telephone call to

England to speak to me,' she accused shakily. 'I waited and waited for you to come and get me but you didn't want to, did you, Andreas? As your brother Alex was so fond of telling m-me, I was the mistake you had to live with, but never, for one second, did I believe all of his mean rubbish until Nikos died and you took off to Athens to console yourself with another woman!'

CHAPTER SEVEN

THERE, it was out. The one secret she had been hugging inside herself for so long it actually ripped at the tissues of her ravaged senses to tear it free! If she had been less distressed she might have noticed the way his whole stance had frozen.

'I h-hate you for that,' she whispered. 'I will never forgive you for doing that!'

His voice when it came was thick and hoarse. 'Alex— my brother told you I...'

She nodded then wished she hadn't when it set off the whole sick, dizzying feeling again. 'And I might have been stupid enough to fall into your sexual trap again,' she said bitterly, 'but I will never, ever *belong* to you again! Now, just let me pass...'

Pushing him to one side, she fled with a hand pressed to her mouth, glad she'd already checked out the other rooms because it meant she could make directly for a finished bedroom with a bathroom attached.

When it was over and the room eventually stopped spinning she dared to move to the washbasin to freshen her mouth and splash cool water on her face. Everything was so new in the bathroom that even the bar of soap was still sealed in its wrapper. As she turned off the tap she caught a glimpse of her face in the mirror and was shocked to see how dreadfully pale she looked because she felt so tingly and hot. Her shoulders and arms had turned pink, she noticed. If she were back at the hotel she would be loading on the after-sun lotion by now but this bathroom contained only the bare essentials.

A sigh turned her round to stare at the closed bathroom door. She knew she couldn't put it off. She had to go back out there and face him—finish it.

He was standing in front of the open wall of glass again with the rigid set of his back facing the room.

'Max Landreau is my employer and a very good friend but he is not my lover,' she stated, 'and the only reason I am telling you that is if I have been unfortunate enough to conceive a baby I don't want any doubt cast upon who the father is.'

He didn't bother to answer. He didn't even bother to turn. All he did was continue to stand there staring at the view as if it was more interesting than what she'd just said. Anger began to sizzle. It was enough that she deeply resented feeling forced into saying what she had, but to be ignored after saying it was the final straw.

As far as she was concerned she'd said more than enough to earn her freedom. 'I'll wait for you in the car—'

'I did come to get you.'

About to spin away, she stilled to watch as he turned to look at her, his lean strong face hewn from rock against a backcloth of uninterrupted blue.

'Say that again,' she shook out.

'I followed you to England but you refused to see me.'
He gave a flick of a long-fingered hand. 'I was not going
to bring this up but you did, so we might as well deal with
it. It was a difficult period for both of us five years ago and
I knew you needed time to come to terms with…what
happened, but how much time, Louisa?' A sigh wrenched
from him. 'You were grieving, I understood that. I behaved
badly after the funeral. I knew I deserved everything that
you dished out. But to refuse to see or even speak to me?
To keep me hanging around in England like a dog to be
whipped and even after weeks of it to *still* send me packing
as if our years together meant nothing to you at all?'

Lost in confusion, Louisa gave a shake of her head.
'But I didn't refuse to see you.'

'I phoned, I wrote; you refused to answer my calls or
my letters.'

'No,' she denied, not wanting to believe this.

The flat line of his mouth offered up a derisive twist.
'Lie to yourself if you feel you must do, but I know it
happened, *agape mou*, and there is only so much banging
of my head against the brick wall of your unforgiving
nature I could take before I finally let it sink in that it really
was over for us.'

The growing horror that he could be telling her the truth
here really shook her. 'I never knew you had come to
England,' she whispered.

Grim scepticism spun him away again. A different kind
of churning took charge of her stomach as she walked
towards him. 'Andreas,' she said. 'I truly did not know! You
came—to England? No one told me. Who did you speak
to? Why didn't they tell you where I…?'

Enlightenment suddenly began to dawn, dragging her feet to a shuddering halt a couple of steps from his hard, lean, unrelenting stance.

'My parents,' she breathed unsteadily.

Her parents had been so eager to get her away from this island, always resentful of the Markonos wealth and power and the way they believed Andreas had used her that summer. When Andreas had walked away after the funeral he had confirmed every bad thought they'd ever had about him.

And his family had not tried to hide their relief when she had eventually agreed to go back to England. For the best, everyone had said. You both need time to recover from your loss. So she'd given in to pressure and left the island, wanting, needing to get away from everything, not least from what she'd read as his desertion of her when she'd needed him the most.

Suddenly the strength drained from her legs and she pulled out one of the chairs then sank down onto it. By then Andreas had turned again and was studying her face with a hard, cold, unforgiving glitter while she sat there numbly recalling all the heartache and pain she had carried away with her along with the heavy drag of her numbing grief.

'After arriving in England I became…very upset,' she improvised because the truth was so impossible to admit. 'H-hysterical,' only just touched the edge of it. 'The doctor decided it was best that I went away to—to convalesce.'

'You were in hospital…?' The stunned catch in his voice made her flinch.

'More like a private retreat,' she said, unable to look at him because even after five years she still found it difficult to accept how quickly she'd sunk into that dark place inside herself. 'If—*when* you came for me my parents were supposed to tell you where I'd gone! They promised me, they promised…'

Then they'd lied and lied and *lied* in their determination to keep them apart. All those long, bleak, empty days and weeks when she'd waited for him to come and get her. All those 'No, he hasn't made contact' replies when she'd asked the question—asked and *asked*! And she'd been so gently let down, so lovingly pitied…

'You are telling me that your parents lied to me?' Andreas said harshly. 'Why the hell would they want to do that?'

Louisa felt her spine quiver as she drew in a breath. To her the *why* was obvious. 'They didn't like you.'

'We were married!' he raked back. 'Whether they liked me or not should not have come into it! We were man and wife and we had just lost our son! We needed each other! It takes more than dislike to want to keep us apart like that!'

'It w-wasn't just them.' Louisa put her hands up to her face and rubbed at it as if trying to rub away the pain of what she was going to say next. Then she dropped her hands and looked up at him standing there like a rumbling dark mountain threatening to erupt. 'I wrote to you too,' she told him thickly. 'I phoned you here at the family villa and at your office in Athens, only to be told you were out of the country… Did your parents or your brother or your secretary pass on any of *my* messages to you?'

He did not need to answer because she knew that they hadn't. *Now* she knew it but not back then when everyone had been so nice and gentle and careful with her.

Conspiracies. She shivered. Their marriage had been

cunningly manipulated by two families who'd conspired to make it come to an end. Even her visits back to this island had been carefully coordinated to ensure that she and Andreas did not meet.

'What you said about my brother…' Andreas prompted darkly.

'I used to tell you about Alex bating me and you used to just brush it off as sibling jealousy. And you know what?' she said starkly. 'I think you were right. At least Alex was open about what he thought about me, while…' while the rest of them smiled nicely as they stabbed us in the back. 'I knew you blamed me f-for what happened to Nikos—'

'Will you stop staying that?' Andreas sighed. 'I did not blame you!'

'Why not, when I blamed myself?' she choked out. 'And it was my own guilt that they worked on, wasn't it? They used it to let me go on believing that you…'

She couldn't say any more because the tears really were threatening now.

'I have to go and deal with this.' The way he suddenly burst out of his stillness left Louisa blinking as he strode through the archway like a man about to—

Leaping up from her chair, she ran after him. 'Andreas—!'

He was halfway up the steps that led to the lobby when she called him. He stopped but he didn't turn, the full length of his frame stiff with anger.

'Please,' she begged him. 'Don't go off angry like you used to do when you didn't like something!'

'You're upset.'

'Of course I'm upset. So are you! But think about it,' she pleaded. 'Charging off to slay them all isn't going to change anything now!'

'They stole five years from us,' he roughed out hoarsely.

'Yes.' Her voice quivered. But it wasn't only them who'd done that. She was thinking about the woman she'd seen him with—the one part of their conversation earlier he had oh, so carefully edited out!

His wide shoulders flexed inside the blue shirting. 'They reduced us both to complete failures as a husband or wife in our own eyes…'

Louisa had to cover her unsteady mouth.

'And to sitting alone at our son's graveside when we should have been sitting there together…'

Oh, it was all so unforgivably cruel when put like that. 'I suppose they believed it was the best thing for both of us at the time or—'

'You believe that?' He swung round to blister a burning look at her.

'Yes—no!' She gave a helpless shake of her head. 'I don't know what to think—I'm still reeling too much from the shock to think!'

'Well, I am not reeling, so you can leave me to deal with it.' He turned away again.

'By climbing onto your jet plane and flying to England so you can have my parents lined up and shot?' she cried out. 'Well, don't go fighting my battles for me, Andreas. I don't need you to do anything for me any more!'

Wrong thing to say…

Louisa knew it the moment that his shoulders racked up and the air began to crackle. When he turned around, one glance at his face and she knew all the anger inside him and the monstrous feelings of hurt had made a switch to something else.

'I think we have strayed away from the main plot a little,' he murmured, coming back down the steps.

'Meaning what?' she asked warily.

'Meaning that this started out as a discussion about you and me enjoying the exciting wonders of unprotected sex on a hill.'

'Are we about to have another fight about whether I'm pregnant or not?' she sighed out. 'For goodness' sake, one mistake does *not* automatically make a baby!'

Her half-shrieked words echoed off painted walls but he didn't even blink. 'It did with Nikos. One time without protection. One beautiful boy exquisitely conceived. One marriage hastily arranged.'

Louisa closed her eyes and tried to keep a grip on her temper because she knew where this was leading. 'I am not taking up the role of your wife again on the wild off-chance that we've done the same thing again!'

'Wild does not cover it.'

He sounded so close suddenly that she flicked her eyes open, her insides tumbling when she saw just how close he had come. Looking up into his face was like putting your fingers too close to a burning flame—dangerous, she likened as his sheer height and breadth and muscled strength snatched away her breath. Pure self-defence made her ease back from him, her breasts fluttering on an unsteady breath when she found her spine flattened up against the wall.

He followed—lazily, a wide shoulder coming to rest on

the wall to one side of her, a long arm stretching across her to brace the flat of his palm on the wall on her other side, the whole manoeuvre aimed to trap her inside a circle of that oh-so-macho web of leashed power.

'Let us deal with this issue once and for all,' he murmured ever so softly, 'and keep looking at me while we talk, *agape mou*,' he instructed when she shut her eyes again to block it all out. 'I want you to see in my face that I am not playing around here.'

Louisa knew that already. She knew it with every slowly shredding nerve in her body that this was no game. She tried for some air that would help keep her head clear, couldn't help moistening her suddenly dry lips as she lifted her chin and slowly opened her eyes. This close up he was without doubt the most frighteningly gorgeous man she had ever encountered—or ever wanted to encounter, she extended helplessly. One Andreas had always been more than enough for her.

'All right,' wrapping her arms across her breasts, she tried for a careless shrug, 'say what you want to say.'

'You don't want to see blood spilt and I do. So I will make a deal with you.'

'What kind of deal?'

'Be my wife again, in every sense, and I will attempt to control my desire to spill blood.'

'This is silly,' she shot out. 'Why talk about this now when we will *know* one way or another in a couple of weeks if it even needs discussing at all? Once I'm back in England and can buy a testing kit without causing another Markonos scandal to erupt here, of course.' She could not resist the sarcastic tag-on.

'Because it isn't just about the pregnancy now. I want more than that.' He ignored her sarcasm. 'I want my lost five years back.'

Her folded arms tightened. 'You can't have them back, Andreas.'

'Then someone has to pay for their loss.'

'Oh, stop being so disgustingly primitive,' she snapped crossly. 'An eye for an eye, a tooth for a tooth— I thought it was the Greeks who pulled the rest of us *out* of the Dark Ages!'

He smiled at that. 'Quick,' he commended. 'But you will not change my mind. You come back to me or our two families will pay the price.'

Her sensitive stomach turned queasy again. 'I'll give you an answer in a couple of weeks.'

'I can do a lot of damage in a couple of weeks, *agape mou.*'

Her chin shot up. 'Stop calling me *your darling* when you're standing here trying to intimidate and blackmail me!'

'You would prefer me to use other incentives…?'

Eyes spiralling into a darker shade of blue, Louisa didn't need to ask what those other incentives would be. 'I should have known you would bring this right down to its most basic function,' she muttered.

'*Sex,*' he dared to name it, 'now, in one of the furnished bedrooms,' he offered. 'Think about it,' he urged. 'You and me coupling like we used to do, driving each other mad for hours and hours.' Bringing up a hand he gently touched the telling burn in one of her cheeks. 'We could enjoy a whole afternoon of glorious unprotected sex with no interruptions from—'

'What do you mean—*unprotected sex*?'

'I would have thought that was obvious.' He smiled. 'I *want* to make you pregnant.'

Robbed of breath, Louisa stared up at him. 'You mean you actually *want* there to be a baby?'

'I have thought of little else since our wild encounter on the hill,' he admitted candidly. 'Call me broody if you like,' he mocked sardonically, touching the trembling fullness of her mouth. 'I want to plant another seed inside your womb and be around this time to watch it grow.'

'Stop it.' She jerked her head back. 'This is crazy.'

'And it gets worse,' he confessed. 'You see, I began wanting this all the more once the name Max Landreau raised its threatening head. And do you know why?'

Louisa shook her head, not even trying to out-think a madman.

'Because the idea of you conceiving another man's child was just so unacceptable to me you were lucky you were with our son when I came looking for you, or I probably would have strangled you on the mere off-chance that you might be pregnant to another man!'

'My God,' she gasped. 'You are unbelievable!'

'Well, try thinking of it this way round. Ask yourself, my reluctant wife, how you would feel about me seeding my child in another woman…'

It was a blow Louisa had not anticipated. It flattened her back to the wall and whitened her face. 'How did you get to be so brutal?' she whispered.

His hands came up to frame her face, long fingers so incredibly tender as they slid her hair behind her ears. It was an old gesture and a familiar one he had used to make as a form of apology.

'Primitive and brutal I might be but it hurts, hm?' he persisted nonetheless. 'It turns you inside out. My mother threw us together to make us see that we had nothing left between us but she could not have been more wrong if she had tried, because there is plenty left between us. You tremble,' he husked. '*I* tremble because we still feel this much for each other.'

'It's just sex and the shock of what you said,' Louisa dismissed all of that. 'It will pass.'

'But I don't want it to pass.' Lowering his head, he brushed his warm lips across hers.

And her lips clung—they *clung*!

'Think about it,' he urged. 'Think about what we shared on the hill and what is still eating away inside us right here and now. Think of all the loving waiting for us the moment that you say *yes* to me. And think of the brother or sister we will make for Nikos and how happy he will be for us that we found each other again. We have a chance to make something good out of so much badness. All you have to do is agree to stay with me...'

She melted into thick, blinding tears.

Smothering a curse, Andreas wanted to take the words back. He despised himself for saying them at all! But he was not going to take them back because he meant them, every single aching one. They'd been cheated of the right to decide for themselves what happened to their marriage five years ago. They'd been manipulated by people who'd insisted on seeing them as children playing at marriage because they'd been foolish enough to conceive a son. In their twisted wisdom their families had decided that with Nikos gone their hasty young marriage should go too. It infuriated him. It burned like acid in his gut to know that people they believed loved them could do this to them.

Where would they be now without the interference? Who knew the answer? Certainly not him, he admitted as he stood looking down at this woman he had met at the wrong time in both their lives but had never—ever felt any differently about.

His mother wanted closure. Well, he wanted closure—only not in the way his mother had meant. To a Greek possession was everything. To a Greek you did not play around with something as deeply ingrained as that. Louisa belonged to him. He'd known it from the moment she walked off the ferry. What had taken place on the hill had only reinforced that belief. She was his, had always been his and would always be his. It was as simple and as clear as that.

'If those tears spill over I will have to take drastic action,' he warned her.

Pressing her trembling lips together, Louisa inhaled a controlling breath. 'I will not be bulldozed into something I don't want because you need to prove something to everyone.'

'You have not been listening…'

'Yes, I have.' She looked up, eyes still awash with tears. 'You are angry and you want revenge and you want me to be your accomplice.'

He didn't like that. The way he stepped away from her told her that he didn't like it. It was much too close to the truth. 'I simply want back what they took from us.'

The moment he gave her some space to breathe Louisa felt a hot tingle spring out along her arms and shoulders. She rubbed at them absently. 'We are two different people now. It would be like trying to relive a past that just doesn't exist.'

'Are you daring to tell me that our son did not exist?' His sudden burning blast of fury shook Louisa to the core.

'Of course I'm not!' she cried out. 'But you cannot recreate Nikos in another child, Andreas! That's just—'

He went as white as a sheet and walked away from her.

Oh, dear God. Louisa closed her eyes. She should not have said that. Shaking badly inside and out now, she pushed herself away from the wall and tracked after him. He'd gone back into the kitchen and was standing in front of one of the units with his dark head dipped and his shoulders braced and he was holding on to the marble worksurface with a white-knuckled grip.

'I'm sorry,' she said. 'It was a terrible thing for me to say.'

'Some terrible things have been said all round,' he uttered with an odd dry rasp. 'It is what comes of waiting five years to say most of them.'

'Yes,' Louisa sighed out. 'But two wrongs don't make a right, Andreas. Surely you must see that?'

'No, I do not see that.'

'Stubborn,' she mumbled, forced to switch her attention from their fight to herself because she'd put a hand up to her forehead and discovered it was burning hot, yet she was starting to shiver she felt so cold.

'I am going to make coffee. Do you want some?' he asked calmly, as if it was perfectly normal to drink coffee in the middle of a heated argument.

An odd-sounding laugh surged up from her throat. 'Actually,' she heard herself say almost curiously, 'I don't think I feel very well…'

CHAPTER EIGHT

AT LEAST it brought him round to face her, she noticed hazily as both he and the room began to fog in and out. There was a moment of complete stillness followed by a curse and a dizzying blur of movement before her hand was snatched away from her forehead so that Andreas could place his hand there instead.

'You are burning up!' he exclaimed. 'Why didn't you say something?'

'We were too busy fighting.'

The next rash of curses rattled in his throat as he lifted her off her feet.

'Put me down,' she protested. 'I'm not so ill I can't walk!'

'Shut up,' he gritted, striding for the steps to the lobby.

'I've got a terrible headache,' she confessed on a groan. 'And I'm all hot but I can't stop sh-shivering.'

'It is called sunstroke,' he clipped out in disgust. 'Do you feel nauseous?'

She nodded. 'Been sick once already. Sorry,' she added and let her head droop onto his shoulder and hated herself for feeling so good about being able to put it there. A few seconds later and the soft feel of a bed arrived beneath her with the cool touch of fine linen that made her shiver all the more.

'Look at your shoulders and your arms,' he said angrily.

'They're just a bit hot.'

'You need a doctor—'

'Oh, that's right,' Louisa sighed out, 'bring in Dr Papandoulis and let's start that great scandal you were so concerned about, when he discovers your estranged wife lying in the bed you usually reserve for your stupid mistresses!'

'Parakaló?' He straightened up with a violent jerk.

'You might well beg my pardon!' she shivered out, feeling so cold now she just wanted to crawl beneath the pale blue bed covers and curl up in a tight little ball. 'The last magazine I saw with you splashed across it you had some lush little starlet hanging on to you like a limpet as you set off for your *island retreat!*'

'I don't bring women here.' Blood surged into his taut face as he said it.

Not believing him, Louisa wanted to hit him. Then she suddenly shot upright and to her feet as another thought hit her full-on.

'Did you sleep with *her* in this bed…?'

She was staring at the bed in horror.

'No— You—'

'Is that why you've had this villa built—so that you can bring your women here? Keep them separate from *the family*?' She was becoming hysterical and she knew it but just didn't care! 'No wonder this place is barely furnished— you only needed a bed! Did you ever have cause to bring Dr Papandoulis out to one of them while they lay sick here?'

'Louisa, you—'

'Don't speak to me.' Shaking as well as shivering now, she continued, 'Y-you've already said enough. How dare you demand the last five years back when within weeks of deserting me you were shacked up with some woman while I hid and wept?'

He'd gone from red to white in as many seconds. '*Agape mou*, don't—'

'I can't believe we did what we did on the hill the other night,' she shook out. 'I can't believe I let you touch me at all after I've had to read every rotten detail of every rotten other woman you've been with in the last five years!'

'It was not like that—' He reached for her.

'Don't touch me!' She pulled back. 'I don't feel well. I w-want to go h-home.'

'You're not well enough to go anywhere,' he told her anxiously.

'Well, I am not getting into that bed!'

'*Theos!*' he exploded. 'The bed is new!' Leaning past her, he tossed the pale blue covers back. 'I had it flown in yesterday along with all the other furniture because I knew you would not want to stay with me at the family villa!—This house is not even ready for occupation!' he added tautly as he straightened up again. 'But I thought we could manage with the essentials. And I have *never* brought any woman to this island!' he barked. 'And you should know better than to believe everything you read in some sick glossy rag! Now, get into that bed before I murder you, Louisa!'

With that he turned and slammed out of the room, leaving her to sink weakly down on the bed in a mess of shaken limbs and emotions.

She had not even wanted to say any of that yet it had all

just come pouring out! Fresh shivers overtook her, her burning skin quivering with prickly heat. On a low, angrily frustrated groan she just about managed to remove her skirt and top before she keeled over onto the cool linen then tugged the covers up to her chin. Her head was pounding, her stomach joining in, and hating Andreas for all she was worth only made her wriggle restlessly in the bed, which in turn made her wince when the movement irritated her burnt skin.

As soon as she was feeling fit enough she was getting out of here, she vowed fiercely. And he could take his lousy revenge-ridden proposition *and* his philandering self and offer them to some other woman—a woman who was probably as overused as him!

'Here,' a stiff voice prompted.

Peeling her heavy eyes open, Louisa discovered Andreas standing over her like some dark entity.

'What?' she mumbled aggressively.

Nothing flickered on his hard mask of a face as he held a glass out towards her. 'To help the dehydration,' he said.

Sending the liquid in the glass a dubious look, Louisa pulled herself up and took it from him.

'And this…' His open palm showed her a small pill. 'Antihistamine to help cool your blood and take the sting out of your sunburn,' he explained in the retracted tone of someone in no mood to take another argument.

'I'm not sure if I should be taking…'

'I checked with a doctor friend in Athens,' he inserted. 'The antihistamine might make you drowsy but it will not be harmful in any other way.'

He meant to a baby if there was one, though he was

being very careful not to use the word now. Clearly, she'd shaken him up when she'd spat all of that out about his other women, so now he was playing it cold and stiff.

'Thanks,' she muttered and grudgingly took the pill from him then swallowed it down with the drink.

The drink tasted a bit odd but wasn't too unpleasant. Handing the glass back to him, she sank down on the pillows, rolling carefully onto her side so she wasn't facing him, then tugged the covers up over her burning shoulders and shut her eyes.

He did not move. Tension began to zip around them. Louisa had a feeling he was still standing there because he had something he wanted to say.

Well, she did not want to hear it.

'Go away,' she husked, desperately wanting to shiver and shake and put in a few miserable groans but refusing to let herself give in to the need while he stood there.

First she heard his heavy sigh, then the sound of his footsteps taking him back to the door, and absurdly she wanted to burst into tears.

What she did was drop like a stone into a deep slumber.

When next she awoke she was aware of something cool being smoothed into one of her arms. She opened her eyes to find Andreas sitting beside her on the bed, his dark eyes hooded and his mouth very grim.

'Stay calm,' he said as she made to stiffen. 'I am not about to ravish you. I am merely applying a lotion to your burns.'

The effect was so wonderfully soothing that she didn't want to do anything but lie there and let him continue. 'You seem to be prepared for anything,' she said drowsily.

'Mm,' was all he replied. But it was a very sexy *mm*, the

kind of deep-bodied *mm* that vibrated up from his chest then across her senses and made her move restlessly between the sheets.

'Be still.'

He was holding her arm out and was working the cooling lotion into her skin with all the gentleness of a masseuse. Eyes half-shut and still heavy with sleep, she watched him for a little while, unbelievably relaxed and unbelievably contented to just study him while he twisted her arm this way and that. She didn't even mind when he reached the really hot spot on her shoulder though she was wearing no bra and was aware that the covers were slipping lower the higher up he worked.

A grateful sigh eased from her as the lotion began to neutralise the heat. 'You'll get it on the bedding,' she thought she'd better point out when he finally allowed her arm to settle on the bed.

'I would rather ruin the bedding than watch your skin peel off.' He reached across her to pick up the other arm. 'I thought you had learned to be more careful with your fair skin years ago.'

'I used a sun-block before I left the hotel,' she defended. 'I just lost track of the time I'd been out, that's all.'

He glanced up as she looked at him. Their eyes locked and her breathing stilled as a fine electric current began to pass between the two of them. It was sexual, they both knew that. Just as they both knew that if they did not break eye contact this was going to shift to a different all-consuming level.

He broke the eye contact first, his long lashes folding downwards as he twisted his body so he could begin work on her other arm. And because the antihistamine was making her feel like this, she told herself, she closed her eyes and just lay unmoving as he continued smoothing lotion into her until the sexual tug faded and without her knowing it she sank back into a relaxed sleep.

Leaving Andreas to grimace at the nagging sexual tug he was suffering from, which had no intention of relaxing its grip on him. He completed his task by gritting his teeth together before gently easing the cover down a little so he could smooth lotion into the slope of her breasts, where the skin was pink but not hot, he was relieved to discover.

After that he paused for a moment to study her sleeping face with her soft, slightly parted mouth and her dusky eyelashes resting against the delicate bones in her cheeks. Her face had escaped the sun's heat by some miracle but just in case, and with infinite care, he smoothed the lotion into her forehead and her small, straight nose.

When he reached her chin his fingers lingered. Then he grimaced again and bent down to press a kiss to that sleep-softened. too tempting mouth. It quivered as she sighed. He frowned as he straightened and wished the hell he knew what was going to happen next.

Maybe Louisa was right and you couldn't get five years back. Maybe he was crazy to want to try. They had baggage now.

Too much baggage?

Standing up, he walked into the bathroom to wash the lotion from his hands while he pondered that question.

No answer arrived like a bolt of lightning. No wise whisper of advice arrived from the gods. Walking back into the bedroom, he found that she'd moved while he'd been out of the room, her arms flung up on the pillows and her breasts now fully exposed.

Small, high, firm and tightly peaked by tempting pink rosebuds. And the answer to his question came right there. Not from the gods, not from his own head but from her perfectly shaped and very tempting breasts.

This woman, those breasts, that mouth, the fine-boned, slender body and long legs hidden beneath the sheets—all of this belonged to him.

Fight him as she no doubt would, she was going nowhere, he determined.

The next time Louisa awoke it was to the muffled sounds of voices. Sitting up, she pushed her tangled hair back from her face then took a few moments to look around the room while her foggy brain tried to sort out the events of a day that had brought her finally to this bed.

Then the door handle rattled and with a lurch she snatched at the cover and pulled it firmly beneath her arms. A second later and her brother appeared in the doorway—carrying her bags.

'Well, talk about luxury.' Jamie grinned at her. 'Have you seen this place? When it's finished it's going to be the best house on the island!'

Louisa blinked. 'Wh-what are you doing with my bags?'

'Andreas said you were too ill to pack them yourself,' he explained.

Two things hit Louisa at once. One that Jamie was very relaxed about her being here. The other that he seemed to think it was perfectly natural to find her occupying her estranged husband's bed!

'Andreas does not have the right to make that decision,' she said crossly. 'And since when did you become bosom pals with him?'

Jamie gave a shrug, his long frame hunching slightly as he stuffed his hands into the pockets of his jeans and the grin disappeared from his face. 'He told me what the parents did.'

'He did what…?' she gasped out.

'I can't believe they could all be so—'

'He had no right to tell you anything!'

'Well, take that up with him not me,' Jamie said. 'Did you know he's got a brand-new jet-ski out there just waiting for someone to try it out?'

'Jamie!' she said in dismay.

A movement by the bedroom door caught her attention. She found Andreas standing there. 'Pietros is waiting for you,' he said quietly to her brother.

'Oh, yeah, right,' Jamie responded and turned to look at her again. 'I'm off out for a night on the town with Pietros, so Andreas said it was OK for me to stay on at the hotel.'

Andreas said…Louisa looked at the man himself. 'Since when do you make decisions about my brother's sleeping arrangements?'

Jamie looked at her too. 'You're not well, sis. Get your act back together and I'll come and see you tomorrow.'

With that he loped off, all cocky arrogance that further infuriated her when he sent a quick rueful glance at Andreas before leaving an atmosphere behind fit to slice through with a knife.

Andreas was still propping up the doorway, every inch of him as relaxed as a man could be, but Louisa knew it was a front. He was waiting to find out what she was going to say before he decided how to react to it.

And he was still wearing the same pale blue shirt and dark trousers, she noticed, but his hair wasn't so neat. There was a five o'clock shadow darkening his jaw and his eyes might be hooded but she could see a telling glitter lurking behind the heavy lids.

The main door banged shut behind her brother, the sound echoing right through the house. She moved—Andreas didn't—and her gaze drifted over to where Jamie had placed her bags. By the look of them, everything she had brought with her to Aristos had been packed up and transported here.

She transferred her gaze back to Andreas. 'Would you like to explain to me what you've told my brother to turn him into your best friend?'

'The truth,' he said.

'Your version,' she derided that.

'It is still the truth,' he countered with a shrug. 'I refuse to have any more lies spoken about us or by us.'

'And I have no say in that, of course.'

'None that I can think of,' he confirmed. Then it was his turn to release a sigh. 'Leave Jamie out of this, Louisa,' he advised soberly. 'He does not deserve to be dragged into it.'

'And your family, are they to be dragged into it? Are we about to receive a visit from them so that I can tell them how they've been sussed as manipulating liars?'

'My parents are no longer on the island,' he informed her, 'They flew back to Athens this afternoon—at my request.'

'You mean you're big enough to bully them too now?'

'Yes,' he hissed out, his patience suddenly waning. 'We

have ourselves to sort out before we even start to think about anybody else's feelings.'

'Well, that's a big turnaround from wanting to spill blood!'

His squared chin jutted. 'I've calmed down.'

Lucky you, she thought because she wasn't feeling calm at all! 'And I've been abandoned—again,' she sighed, sinking back against the pillows.

'I am still here.'

'You,' she flicked at him, 'are the problem.'

'Such an exciting problem though,' he dared to grin, 'so stop complaining and tell me how you feel.'

It was when he walked across to the bed and picked up an iced jug of water that a feeling of him having done this before filtered into her head. She went still, blue eyes narrowing as she watched him pour water into a glass then offer it to her.

'Sit up and drink,' he instructed.

Flashbacks of being woken up and made to do this several times during the afternoon hit her head, followed by another set of images—of Andreas sitting beside her gently smoothing lotion into her heated skin. That old feeling of awareness shot into play with a vengeance. Her breasts began to grow tight, a telling dampness spreading across a place that made the hairs around it prickle as they stirred in response.

Sitting up very slowly, she took the glass from him. She was beginning to remember all kinds of things that had taken place during the afternoon, like the brush of his mouth on her mouth. Her cheeks began to heat as she sipped the cool water. How far had he actually gone while she'd been comatose? She remembered talking to him, though not what she'd said. She remembered lying here enjoying the soothing stroke of his touch.

Had she allowed him to do more than that? Had she—?

'Kostas has just delivered my clothes here,' he remarked with no idea as to where her thoughts had gone off to. 'I am in need of a shower. Do you want to use the bathroom before I take it over?'

'Can't you use another room?' Louisa handed the glass back, refusing to look at him in case his expression told her things she did not want to know.

'This is my bedroom,' he countered smoothly. 'And that is my bed.'

'I'll get out of it, then…' she was about to throw back the covers when she remembered she was wearing nothing other than the tiniest pair of white cotton panties. Sheer frustration ripped a sigh from her as she sank back again.

'Maybe I should rephrase that,' her tormentor murmured softly. 'This is *our* bedroom, and that is *our* bed.'

Something lazy about his tone had her lifting her eyes to look at him, only to wish that she hadn't when she saw the mocking humour lighting his velvet dark eyes because it showed he knew exactly what she had been thinking about.

But worse, she saw he'd unbuttoned his shirt while she hadn't been looking, and now the pale blue cloth hung open to reveal a long strip of bronzed torso with its impressive muscular structure and arrowhead of virile dark hair.

Dragging in a tense, stifled breath, he said, 'I want you—'

'I know you do…' Deliberately waylaying what she had been about to say, he swooped low and captured her mouth so fast all she managed was a protesting gasp.

He smothered the sound with warm, gentle kisses laid like promises along her soft lips, one set of long fingers threading into her silk hair so he could hold her still. He badly needed to shave and the rasping brush of stubble against her skin made her quiver and, like the fool she always was around him, she lifted her arms up to encircle his neck and started kissing him back.

His low grunt of satisfaction should have annoyed her but it didn't. When he sat down on the bed so he could draw her up against him the sheet slithered down to her waist, exposing her breasts to the full impact of his warm naked chest. Heat sizzled across her cooling skin like a second dose of sunburn, making her move in a restless wriggle that sent the wanton tips rasping against the prickly hairs on his chest. He responded by spreading his hands across her naked back and arching her closer so her head tilted backwards and on a hungry growl he deserted her mouth to trail a string of hot kisses down her throat and over both creamy slopes until he finally claimed a tight, eager nipple and took it deep into his mouth.

It wasn't fair was the last sensible thought she had as she melted into a puddle of exotic sensation. She wanted him but she didn't want to. She wanted to push him away but what she did was score her nails down his back beneath his shirt in encouragement. He shuddered and came back to plunder her mouth with hot and earthy driving passion.

Then, as if he were some evil torturer, he just let go of her and shot like a bullet to his feet, leaving her to fall back against the pillows, gasping for breath and quivering with shock.

'Why?' she breathed, so shaken up by his desertion she could barely make the single word work.

'We still have issues to deal with.' As if he needed to do something physical he dragged his shirt off and tossed it aside. Seeing the red score marks from her nails marking his muscular contours flooded Louisa with guilty heat. 'Falling on each other like a pair of uncontrolled teenagers only confuses things.'

Snaking upright, Louisa reached for the sheet and dragged it up to her neck with shaking fingers, almost suffocating in self-loathing that she hadn't thought to do it before.

'Maybe the uncontrolled stuff is all we ever had going for us,' she retaliated bitterly. 'It was always like that for us, wasn't it? You would go away for weeks on end then either come back here to the island or have me transported to Athens so we could fall on each other for a day or two before you'd be off somewhere else.'

'It was not like that.' His bronzed shoulders moved in a tight, masculine flex as he turned away again.

'It was exactly like that,' Louisa insisted, hating herself for always being so easy for him! 'And I was so stupidly naïve I thought it had to mean that you must really love me to want me so much, but really it was just the great sex you enjoyed and you probably continued that elsewhere with someone else!'

He slammed into the bathroom and Louisa knew it was because he could not deny it, especially when she had seen him for herself! Now she wanted to cry. She wanted to squirm in shame at her lack of control—again—even *knowing* he was such a low-down, faithless rat!

CHAPTER NINE

SHE was not going to cry, Louisa told herself fiercely as she got off the bed with a quivering stretch of angry limbs. Discovering that she was not very steady on her feet did not help the way she was feeling.

The antihistamines must still be in her system, she assumed as she made her way over to her bags. Squatting by the big canvas holdall, she rummaged inside for something to wear, came out with a little top with thin straps that should not rub her sunburn, found a short cotton skirt, fished out fresh underwear and her soap bag then took herself off to the other furnished bedroom to take a shower.

As she stepped out of the bedroom she spied another holdall standing against the lobby wall. It was a big black expensive-looking leather thing that had Andreas stamped all over it. The urge to give it a good kick almost got the better of her as she stalked past it on her way to the other bedroom.

Then she suddenly stopped to look at the front door as another thought struck her: why wasn't she stamping and screaming to be taken back to the hotel? The honest answer to that question promised to be so demoralising that she decided not to let it form in her head.

With the grim knowledge that hiding from herself was the fools way to deal with all of this, she stepped beneath the shower and let the stinging spray hitting her tight hot skin punish her for being so weak and gullible.

Standing beneath the shower spray, Andreas waited for the stinging cold water to freeze the nagging ache from his loins. He must have been mad to call a halt to what they had been doing. Perhaps the sexual fog had been a safer place to sink into than trying to deal with *issues* he'd discovered he did not want to deal with at all.

Which said what to him?

That maybe she was right and the sex was all they had left going for them. That it was all they'd ever had?

No. Slamming a hand against the shower dial, he switched the spray from cold to hot and began to wash. He refused to believe that. It would be like admitting that their families had been right about them all along.

OK, then fight your own corner, he told himself. You are supposed to be the man who can talk a whole boardroom of doubters round to your way of thinking, so do it now. Clear your head and deal with the issues that really matter.

Not the sex, though the sex was still the gut-twisting ache it had always been when he was anywhere near her.

Not their interfering families, though they were still going to pay for what they'd done no matter how things turned out between them here.

And then there was that other issue out there still waiting to be dealt with.

Max Landreau.

Snatching up the shampoo bottle he squeezed some onto the palm of his hand.

Did she think he would not recognise the name of the tall, dark, handsome media tycoon? Landreau had a long reputation with women. He collected them as other men would collect stamps! Was she naïve enough to believe he wouldn't bother to check their relationship out?

Give him twenty-four hours and he would have some answers, but right now, standing here rubbing shampoo into his hair, thoughts of *any* man being intimate with *his wife* was threatening to eat him alive.

By the time Louisa stepped back into the hall, the black leather bag had disappeared and the door was firmly shut. Fingering the ends of her wet hair, she hovered for a moment. She wanted to get her hair-dryer, but if Andreas was still there she had no wish to walk in on yet another round of arguments.

In the end she took herself down the steps and into the kitchen. No matter how much liquid Andreas had been pouring into her throughout the afternoon she was still thirsty—and hungry too. Putting the kettle to boil so she could make herself some fresh coffee, she raided the fridge and came out with enough food to make herself a sandwich. By the time she'd done that the coffee was ready, pouring herself a cupful, she even began to relax a little as she took the cup and her sandwich over to the table and was about to sit down when her attention was drawn to the plate-glass window standing invitingly open to the soft golden blush of the late afternoon.

It was just too irresistible. Taking her prepared snack

with her she walked outside so she could take a proper look at the view. The house was situated in its own small cove, with the sinking sun now hanging above a glass-smooth ocean. Picking her way carefully over what was still mostly a building site, she made her way to the edge of the shingle beach then paused to glance around.

She did not recognise the spot, though she couldn't understand why she didn't when, on her first trip to the island, Andreas had made it his business to take her to every secluded beach there was, even those that could only be reached by the sea. Glancing back at the house, she saw that it nestled gently into a thicket of tall pine trees. It was much bigger when viewed from this position, she realised, its modern frontage a series of plate-glass windows set at different angles to gain the most from the ocean view. One of which must belong to the bedroom she'd been sleeping in, though she'd barely noticed it had a window, she'd been feeling so ill.

Turning around again, she spotted a low, flat projection of rock sticking out of the ground and went to sit down on it to sip at her coffee and eat her sandwich.

The cicadas were busy, the air filled with the scent of olives and pine and the sea. Tucked into a corner of the beach beneath a tree was the bright red jet-ski Jamie had mentioned and—

'So what do you think?'

The sound of his deep voice from behind her stiffened her shoulders out of their nicely relaxed droop. 'Am I supposed to have an opinion?'

He had not built this for them after all—which then fed her the question, who had he built it for? Not liking where that thought was taking her, she took a sip of her drink.

'If you are genuinely not interested,' he drawled easily, 'then by all means continue to be a grouch.'

Then he caught her thoroughly unawares when he came to sit down on the rock behind her, spreading his long legs either side of hers. Warm, tanned, hair-roughened thighs appeared in her vision. For a wildly staggered heartbeat she thought he'd come out here wearing nothing until she caught sight of the edges of a pair of cargo shorts and the short sleeves of a pale blue T-shirt moulding his muscled upper arms as he reached round her to place an ice bucket by her feet, containing an opened bottle of champagne.

The clean, tangy scent of him blocked out the scent of olive and pine and she pulled in a deep breath and arched her spine in an effort to place a distance between the two of them.

'If the house was one of our new cruise ships we would be breaking the champagne bottle on her hull,' he said lightly. 'Since it is a house and not a ship, I thought we would drink the champagne instead.'

Next thing he'd looped his hands beneath her arms and produced two champagne flutes.

'Get rid of the plate and the coffee cup and take these from me,' he instructed.

One part of her wanted to get up and walk away from him but another part was still stinging from being called a grouch.

'This is so romantic.' She restricted herself to a touch of acid as she gave in and took the glasses.

He ignored her and said, 'Hold them upright if you don't want champagne on your skirt.'

Tilting the flutes into an upright position, Louisa watched as he poured champagne until it fizzed and frothed. 'I don't think I should be drinking this on an empty stomach.' She'd barely touched her sandwich.

'A few sips won't make you fall flat on your face.'

You can, though, she thought bleakly.

Taking one of the glasses from her, he chinked it against the other one. 'To us and our new home,' he said and lifted the glass to his mouth and drank.

Louisa didn't drink—not to an *us* that just was not going to happen or the *our new home* bit. 'How is it that I don't remember this spot?' She diverted the subject.

'The land has belonged to me since my grandmother died,' he informed her. 'But the trees used to come to the edge of the shingle until last winter when a storm brought a lot of them down.'

'Making the perfect clearing on which to build a house. Lucky you.'

'Am I not?' was the very dry reply which came back. 'I suppose you are now thinking that I called up the storm so that I could clear the land.'

'I wouldn't put it past you,' she said, remembering the law prohibiting building on Aristos unless it was to replace old with new.

'There used to be an old shed where the house stands but—'

'It blew down in the storm too.'

'You have become a terrible cynic, Louisa,' he chided. 'And here I am, mistakenly thinking that you would find this particular spot so romantic…'

It hit her then, just where it was they were sitting. A stinging sensation shot down the length of her spine and snatched at her breath. 'It isn't…' she whispered.

'We anchored offshore and swam in,' he confirmed. 'I found an old blanket in the hut and we stretched out on the beach in the sun to…dry out.'

Louisa saw it all in vivid Technicolor. Her, lying there in her little pink bikini. Andreas, in his creamy shorts that had such a sexy habit of riding too low on his hips. He'd been teasing her about something—she couldn't remember what—then the teasing had stopped abruptly when he'd rolled over her and suddenly captured her mouth.

She moved restlessly, not wanting to remember the deep, drugging kisses that had grown more and more intimate, or the soft gasps of their fevered breathing as the whole thing had sunk them both beyond the point of pulling back. She could even feel the pebbles digging into her when she'd finally allowed him the one intimacy she had been holding back from him, hear the roughness of his voice groaning, *'I don't want to hurt you,'* and her own helpless whisper, *'You could never hurt me,'* then the full, burning heat of his first powerful thrust.

The muscles around her sex curled then throbbed and tightened, jolting her like a wayward dart to her feet. Behind her she could feel Andreas's surprised stillness. In front of her the sun was setting like a great ball of flaming heat and her heart was pounding, she was shaking all over, her legs had gone hollow except for the shooting stings of telling heat.

She tried to crush it, to damp it all back down again. It was mad that such an old memory should be this intense. She was no longer that innocent seventeen-year-old giving herself for the first time to the man she loved, she was a mature woman with the bitterness of failure and the tragedy of loss to cool her ardour and she no longer loved him—she didn't.

The champagne flute was suddenly snatched from her fingers, hard hands spun her about. She looked into glinting black eyes and trembled all the harder when she saw the fierce reflection of her own wild thoughts stamped into his hard, dark face. Her breathing fractured. He roughed out a thick, damning sound then his hands were tightening.

'No,' she whimpered.

'Yes,' he hissed and wrapped her against him so tightly her head whirled at the raw, hard evidence of his passion as he claimed her mouth with a hot, hunting hunger that hurled the past out there into the sunset and replaced it with the right here and now.

And her surrender to it was so fast she groaned and quivered, despising herself even as the sensual claim of his tongue between her lips sent a burn of pure sensation spearing right down her front and she was kissing him back as if there would be no tomorrow, fighting to get her arms free from his crushing embrace so she could throw them around his neck.

He saved her the trouble by scooping her up in his arms to begin carrying her back to the house. This kiss didn't ease up as he picked his way over the rough ground and entered the kitchen with the sure-footedness of a man arrogant enough to be that confident in himself.

Only when they entered the bedroom and he let her feet slither to the floor did a brief glimpse of sanity return and she wrenched her mouth free. 'What happened to sorting out the issues?' she said on a shaky last-ditch attempt to redeem herself.

'I was wrong.' Deft fingers dealt with the zip holding her skirt up. 'This needs dealing with before we can hope to discuss anything else with cool sense.'

'The *sex*, you mean.' The skirt slithered to the floor around her feet. 'Whenever did it *not* take priority between us?'

As he was about to relieve her of her top something hard flashed across his features. 'Don't ever tell me again that what we had between us was just sex! What we had down there on the beach that just tied you up in sensual knots simply recalling it was special. And if it wasn't for your sunburn I would be ravishing you again out there on those same damn pebbles to remind you how special it was!'

'Even special sex is still just sex, Andreas.'

'Is it?' Her top came off over her head. 'Then, *yineka mou*, let us have *sex*.'

She'd walked herself right into that one, Louisa acknowledged helplessly as with a lithe dexterity he manoeuvred her onto the bed, his kiss already making good its declaration as he followed her down, ravishing the tender interior of her mouth.

And it just went on and on until she was dizzy with it, her fingers agitatedly kneading the thick, muscular shape of his shoulders trapped inside his T-shirt until it wasn't enough.

'Take it off,' she said, dragging her mouth free, her urgent fingers already searching out the edge of the shirt so she could push it up.

Snaking upright he did as she bade him, leaving her spread out on the bed while he stripped off his clothes, watching her watch him as each new inch of sleekly honed, fabulous flesh was exposed to her soft, dark, hungry blue gaze.

He had the strong-boned, handsome face of an arrogant

Greek emperor and the body of an Olympian athlete, she observed breathlessly. So big, so lean, so beautifully presented she couldn't prevent her limbs from enacting a sensual squirm of invitation as he stripped off the shorts to reveal his full formidable strength.

'I should have locked you up in a box years ago,' he muttered as he looked down at her lying there like a golden offering. 'When did you get to be so blatant about what you want?'

'You taught me,' she said and watched his response flare like lightning in his eyes as he came back to her.

'As long as it was only me,' he growled.

There was a single split-second when Louisa wanted to pick up that comment, then he was burying his mouth in her creamy throat and the moment was lost in the hot, deep, sensual journey of his mouth anointing her skin with warm, moist, gliding kisses on his way to her breasts. She released a soft cry and arched beneath him as he claimed a tight, rosy nipple, fingernails biting into his nape as he suckled and teased with his tongue and his teeth until she could bear the pleasure of it no longer and grabbed at his hair to pull up his head.

His eyes were as black as midnight, his skin the colour of sun-warmed bronze, smooth and sleek and sensationally tight.

'Tell me what you want,' he demanded.

'You know,' she groaned, running restless fingers over him and loving the way he flexed and shuddered then took the other breast like a marauding pirate, raiding the eager pink tip until she writhed like a wild thing beneath him. Then he came back to raid her mouth, one set of long fingers searing into her gold silk hair to keep her still while the other set stroked and teased in a torment of expert caresses until he reached the soft, springy curls at her thighs. The kiss broke as he delved deeper, his dark eyes intense on her as he watched her whole length stretch out on a sensation-packed sigh.

He aroused her with smooth, slow, expert patience until she was swollen and wet and he was trembling, a long, sleek mass of passionate male holding her trapped by his weight and the knowing stroke of his fingers as she fought what he was trying to make happen to her. He delved deep into her warm gasping mouth, he suckled the soft fullness of her lower lip. He moved with her and on her, every powerful inch of him playing its part to drive the whole thing on. The tight peaks of her breasts throbbed to his kisses. She scored her nails into his back and into his hair, she gripped the bunched muscles in his arms, latched hungrily on to a taut, muscled shoulder and ran hunting fingers down between them to capture the hard, jutting column of his sex.

'Please,' she whispered, 'please…'

He shuddered on a wave of violent pleasure yet still he held it—controlled it and her, stretching out the fabulous torture until with a suddenness that took her by surprise, he came between her thighs and, on a whispered hot curse, thrust his full length into the morass of sensitised flesh she had become.

No part of her missed out on the glory of it. It swept through her in a wild, heated shimmer from her hair roots to the tips of her toes. No part of him missed out as she moved with him, her arms wrapped around his shoulders, her legs wrapped round his waist. His hands were kneading her hips and her buttocks, his mouth hot with urgency as he suckled her lips. When her explosive cry came with the first rippling wave of climax he let the helpless sound spring around the room and watched with fiercely possessive, glinting black eyes as she lost herself in its screaming-pitch power. Then he joined her, a long, sleek assembly of rippling male muscle taking the reward for his patience in those final grinding surges that spurred her own pleasure on and on.

Afterwards was like floating above the planet, Louisa didn't even feel the need to breathe. Yet he was hot and heavy on her, a golden-skinned weight still experiencing the aftershocks of what they had shared with his strong arms wrapped around her and her legs still wrapped around him.

It felt like an age before he released his grip on her and levered himself up, tender fingers combing the damp strands of her hair from her face. 'Now that,' he kissed her softly, 'was a lot more than just sex...'

Opening her eyes, Louisa looked into the cavern-darkness of his and quivered out a rueful smile. 'In a dominant-male kind of way.'

An ebony silk eyebrow lifted. 'You preferred me to be subservient?'

Lifting her hand, she let her fingers trace the silk arch as she slowly shook her head. She loved the way he took such masterly control of her. He knew that. She loved the way, when he finally surrendered his own control, he did not hold anything back.

'Then why the pensive look?' he questioned.

'Because,' she said, only to stop and frown while she tried to decide what the *because* actually was.

Drifting her eyes over his face, unaware of the stretching silence, Louisa tugged in a breath then wished that she hadn't when that old familiar scent of his loving curled through her senses. Andreas, she thought bleakly, her first lover, her *only* lover. The man she had spent five long years trying hard to forget, yet, as she lay here with him heavy on her, she had to ask herself now how she had managed to exist so long without him when it had taken hardly any time at all to bring them back to this point.

'Not sure you enjoyed it?'

The silken purr in his voice brought her eyes into focus to discover that his had narrowed, the darkened softness of sensual satiation gone from his face.

'You know it was fantastic,' she told him drily.

'No.' He shook his dark head. 'You still look uncertain, so I think we had better try again, only slower this time— perhaps draw out the agony a bit longer until you beg me even more?'

Louisa tensed beneath him. 'I did not beg!' she objected.

'You begged,' he repeated, 'but clearly it was not good enough to stop you from going wherever it was you just wandered off to.'

'I did not wander off anywhere,' she denied in exasperation. 'What's the matter with you, Andreas? You never used to be unsure of your mighty prowess!'

The corners of his mouth flexed. 'Perhaps I'm losing my touch—'

'I think you've gone crazy!'

If the black jealousy burning a hole in his chest was crazy then that, Andreas decided, was what he was.

He knew what it was that was bothering him—Max

Landreau, Andreas thought grimly. Had Louisa been daring to think about Landreau while she lay here beneath him looking all pensive and bleak? Had she been comparing the old lover with the new?

Louisa gave a push at his chest. 'Let me up,' she instructed, stunned by how quickly he'd turned the most amazing loving of her life into another battle—and all because she'd let herself think!

'Not a cat in hell's chance.' He caught hold of her hands and pinned them to the bed.

'I don't like you in this mood,' she gasped, wriggling beneath him.

'You love me in this mood,' he drove her back onto the pillows with the bruising hot pressure of his kiss, 'dominant and primitive and giving you no options. A few days of this and you will be so much my woman again you won't want to wander off anywhere.'

Her eyes widened. 'What do you mean—a few days of this?'

'Well, you are not exactly fighting to get away from me…'

It was a taunt that hit right at her pride and her ego because she wasn't trying to get away—not from this villa, not from this bed…not from him.

Chagrin turned her sparking eyes a deeper shade of blue.

'I am going to love watching you fight the next battle with yourself when the ferry comes back in…'

It took a few seconds for his meaning to click then she sparked all over again. 'If you're daring to think I'm going to stay on here with you after this week then—'

Too late—too late, she thought as he crushed the protest from her lips and the breath from her body. Heat flared in the pit of her abdomen as thirty seconds later and true to his dominant promises he was sinking her right back down into the whole hot, sensual quagmire and to fight him she knew she had to *want* to, but she didn't.

It was her biggest crime, though she chose not to recognise it.

CHAPTER TEN

DAYLIGHT came with glinting droplets of sunlight seeping in through the window and across the bed. Louisa lay there for a few minutes feeling much too lazy to want to bother to move—until it suddenly occurred to her that if the sun had reached such an angle in the sky that it could seep in through the bedroom window then it had to be getting very late.

She sat up in the bed, pushing her tumbled hair back from her face, then groaned as each movement brought on a series of aching complaints. Three days of playing Andreas's sex slave was beginning to take its toll, she noticed drily. They made love, they ate, they made love, they lazed or played in the sun—they made love, she listed with a half-deriding smile. The only respite from this very specialised diet was when Andreas shot off to the family villa for a couple of hours each morning to use the business facilities set up there so he could keep in touch with the outside world.

Or the real world, she amended as she climbed off the bed, because this world wasn't real by any stretch of the imagination. Even her brother was playing his part in the fantasy by making himself scarce as he enjoyed himself with

Pietros while they—well they were behaving like a pair of young lovers pretending the past hadn't taken place at all.

How had she allowed that to happen?

She hadn't. Andreas had, in his arrogant, pushy, dominant role. He had orchestrated her every thought and feeling and action and she had just let him have his way because…

There it was again, she thought on a sigh as she stepped beneath the shower spray, the *because* was still playing games with her head. Only, three days on from the first time she'd stuck on the word, she now had the answer.

She loved him—*still* loved him, and if it had not gone away before now then it was never, ever going to go away, was it? He was so much in her blood he was like a virus, unshakeable and tenacious.

And today the ferry came back.

Stepping out of the shower, she wrapped a towel around her then just sank onto the edge of the bath.

Decision time…

Did she catch the ferry and leave here or did she stay? With him.

On the wild off-chance and flimsy excuse that she might be carrying his child again?

Heaving in a deep breath, she let it back out because that excuse no longer had anything to do with what the two of them had been doing here. They hadn't even discussed the subject of babies again, and Andreas had been very careful to protect her since that first crazy loss of control. In fact they had not discussed anything. He had not asked about her life in London. He had dropped the subject of Max. And their parents were never mentioned. He went quiet sometimes, distant, usually when he returned from the other villa and seemed to struggle to slip out of his businessman role. He even looked different then, distant and cool, as if he'd pulled on a hard outer casing she was not able to penetrate.

The tough tycoon playing the tough tycoon, she likened with a smile.

Then right out of nowhere he would just crash through that outer casing, gather her up and take her to bed, or if he found her lazing on the beach he would strip off, catch hold of her and stride with her into the sea in playful mood—then take her to bed.

The two faces of Andreas Markonos, she mused. The tough and the playful—both were too deliciously charismatic for her peace of mind.

None of which helped her to look beyond the moment when the ferry sailed back in. Getting up, she walked into the bedroom, only to pull to another stop when she saw her bags standing there still lined up against the wall, saying more about the temporary nature of what she was doing here than anything else did.

What happened when she picked up those bags to leave here?

An image of Andreas striding off in one direction while she walked off in the other sent a cold little shiver chasing down her spine. She huddled into the towel. Her life was in England. Andreas's was in Greece. She was no longer the young girl she had used to be, willing to play the placid little wife while he shot off to do the important bread-winning stuff. She had a life, a job she loved and a sense of her own value that had come to mean a lot.

Frowning, she chose fresh clothes out of her now depleted selection, dressed and dried her hair. She'd just stepped into the kitchen when the sound of a jet-ski had her glancing outside to witness the flourishing way her brother guided the craft up the shingle beach.

Looking tall and tanned and rakishly sea-sprayed, he strode up to the house. 'Hi,' he said as he stepped into the kitchen, then sent a quick look around. 'Where's Andreas?'

'Using the office at the other house,' she answered casually.

'Good. That makes it easier because he turns to stone when I mention your boss.'

'You had no right to bring Max up at all,' Louisa said crossly.

'I know, but at the time I enjoyed watching him suffer.' Jamie grinned, unrepentant. 'Anyway, Max is why I'm here. He rang the hotel this morning looking for you. He was *not* pleased when I said where you were.' Digging his hand into the pocket of his shorts, he pulled out a folded slip of paper and handed it to her. 'He wants you to ring him pronto, something urgent.'

Looking down at the note, Louisa unfolded it. 'Switch your damn mobile on!' Jamie had scored with a flamboyant mimic of how Max must have relayed the message to him. 'I have to speak to you—now!'

'But he knows I switch off my phone when I come here.' She frowned.

Jamie just shrugged. 'He sounded very pushy.'

Still frowning, Louisa turned and walked back through the house to the bedroom, wondering what crisis could have erupted at work to put Max in such a bad mood? It wasn't like him, Max thrived on crises. In the four years she'd worked for him he had never attempted to intrude on her vacations with hot little missives like this.

Jamie followed her, obviously too curious to know what the emergency was about to just shoot off again. He leant against the bedroom doorframe to watch as she fished her mobile phone out of her bag and switched it on. An instant flurry of text messages and voice mails tumbled into her inbox—all from Max.

Ignoring them, she hit quick-dial. The moment she made the connection, Max's voice was burning her ear. 'What the hell is going on, Louisa?' he demanded furiously. 'I thought it was over between you and your ex.'

'Max, I don't know what you—'

'I am in the process of being stalked, my business interests picked over like chicken bones. My private life is being probed—by Andreas Markonos!'

Louisa closed her eyes and sank down onto the edge of the bed. 'No,' she gasped. 'You have to be mistaken, Max. Andreas wouldn't—'

'Old skeletons are suddenly falling out of my cupboards and threatening to talk to the tabloids if I don't get rid of you, so don't try to tell me that Markonos is not responsible. What I want to know is why!'

Holding her head in her hands, Louisa closed her eyes, struggling to make sense of it all. 'I don't know why,' she whispered.

'In all the years you've worked with me you haven't so much as mentioned his name after your initial interview, and you have been making your annual pilgrimage to his island—clearly this time you decided to enjoy an intimate interlude with your estranged husband too, hm?'

Louisa shot to her feet. 'That's just not true, Max!'

By the door, Jamie straightened his stance.

'So what happened ?' Max wasn't listening. 'Did you decide to taunt him with our relationship and the ruthless bastard decided to respond by trying to ruin me?'

'Stop it,' Louisa said. 'You and I don't have that kind of relationship and you know it. There isn't a tabloid out there that would dare print any sleaze about you, Max—you own most of them! Look, give me a couple of hours and I'll find out what's going on and get back to you.'

She cut the connection, shaking all over.

'What was all that about?' Jamie demanded.

Flicking a paper-white look at him, she said, 'Can you ask Pietros if he can give me a lift to the Markonos villa?'

'Sure,' her bother shrugged, fishing out his mobile, 'but I wish you would tell me what's going on.'

'I'll tell you when I know.' As she turned away her mind was racing, trying to put the pieces of this jumbled jigsaw together. She recalled Andreas playing it quiet and remote each time he came back from the villa and a hot sting of suspicion shot down her spine.

But surely Andreas wouldn't do anything like this. It was just too underhand. This had to be one of his family's doing, she decided and was shocked how relieved she felt to come up with an alternative explanation that acquitted Andreas from blame.

By the time she'd climbed into Pietros's old car, leaving Jamie to take the jet-ski back to the hotel, she'd totally convinced herself that she was on her way to the Markonos villa to break the news to Andreas that his family were playing dirty tricks again. Kostas came out onto the shady veranda as they drove up to the villa's elegantly sprawling white frontage. Thanking Pietros, she climbed out of the car then stood for a few seconds, hovering as she looked at the house, and suffered a deep reluctance to move any closer to it.

She didn't want to go in there, she admitted to herself as she made her feet take her up the wide marble steps towards a smiling Kostas. It was weird how this villa had become the monster of her past in her mind where all her saddest memories resided.

'Is Andreas here?' she asked the old family retainer.

'He is in the study,' Kostos nodded, stepping to one side of the open door so she could precede him inside. 'It is good to see you here again, *kyria*,' he said warmly.

Louisa just smiled and nodded and kept on going, walking on cool, polished sandstone across the spacious hallway that hadn't changed in a single detail since she'd last been here. The door to the study stood firmly closed. Feeling oddly as if she was about to meet her own executioner, Louisa slid her hands down the sides of her short blue cotton sundress before she could bring herself to open the door.

At first glance everything looked exactly the same as it always had whenever she'd come in here. The stylishly designed functional room, which was really the central control room for the Markonos men to wield their power when they were here on Aristos, was lined by a multitude of hi-tech equipment with printers and fax machines and photocopiers cloaked by cedar cabinets. A long row of computer screens flickered away busily, each showing lists from different stock markets across the globe. Everything looked so comfortingly normal in a money-orientated,

power-spinning kind of way and seeing that made some of
her tension ease away.

Andreas was standing with his hips resting against the
huge cedar desk loaded down with its usual stacks of files
and paperwork. He was on the phone rolling out instruc-
tions in Greek. Her Greek had used to be pretty fluent but
he was speaking so fast and intensely she didn't have a
hope of understanding what he was saying.

And anyway she wasn't listening, she was looking.
Even dressed casually in pale chinos and a plain white
shirt, he exuded all the heady dynamics of a hard, polished
tycoon. He was staring at his shoes, frowning, his cropped
hair shining blue-black in the sunlight coming at him from
the window behind him and casting deliciously brooding
dark shadows across his face.

Alpha man relaxing at home, she drily observed. If you
put him on the front page of *Vogue* looking like that the
shops would sell out within minutes of the copies hitting
the shelves. He was gorgeous—sexy; her tummy muscles
flipped over and that hot, telling sting hit her abdomen to
remind her that this was the only man ever to make her
feel like this.

He glanced up and saw her then and surprise froze him,
cutting off his voice as if someone had severed his tongue
from his throat.

'Hi,' she smiled at him, 'I'm sorry to disturb you here
but—'

'You are very welcome to disturb me,' he declared as
he shot bolt-upright. The phone rattled as it landed on its
rest. As he strode quickly towards her everything about
him was jerky and tense. The way he came to stop directly

in front of her filled her with the strangest impression that he was deliberately blocking her off from the desk.

It spooked her enough to send her heart on a sinking dive to her stomach. When he reached out to take hold of her to kiss her, she took a wary step back. Something was wrong here.

'No, don't touch me yet,' she jerked out. 'I need to ask you something first…'

His dark eyes narrowed on her sudden tension. As he lowered his hands to his sides, Louisa watched them ball into two tense fists. When she looked up again it was as though a shutter had been slammed down across his face.

'Ask me what?' he prompted.

And then she knew. It was right there in his body language, in the clenched fists and his shuttered expression and his tense, blocking stance. It had nothing to do with his family—it was him.

She took another step back from him, feeling very cold suddenly, shivering, pins and needles chasing up her legs from the oddly unstable pads of her feet. Her heart began to thump. Eyelashes flickering as she looked away from him, she took a sideways step then just walked around him to go over to the desk.

A tense, dragging silence followed as she stood there moving her stark blue eyes from one stack of papers to the next stack, each one clearly labelled with the name of one of Max's companies. Her name—her *other* name, Louisa Jonson—jumped out at her from a closed folder on the far side of the desk.

The phone started ringing—ringing and ringing, while Andreas held his stillness and the air slowly thickened with that insistent sound slicing through it as if it were trying to slice through her.

Then the phone stopped. Louisa drew in a breath. 'I thought it was your father,' she pushed out unevenly. 'I refused to believe that you would…' Pale as death, she spun around. *'Why?'* she choked out.

His shrug was so insolent it almost hurt her more than all the rest put together. 'Landreau is your lover.'

Louisa stared at him and couldn't push out a single word in denial because he looked so calm, sounded so casual about the accusation that she actually found herself waiting for him to offer another one of those horrible shrugs.

'Nothing to say?' He offered a quick condemning smile instead. 'Very wise,' he added as he strode back to the desk, all lean, lithe, smooth-moving male in complete control of himself.

He reached across the desk to flip open the file with her name on it. 'To give you your due, *yineka mou,*' he continued, 'at least you used your unmarried name while you spent the last four years travelling Europe, passing yourself off as Landreau's assistant.' The last word bit from between his teeth. 'If, however, I can gather this much intimate information about your affair with him so quickly, then how much more could an experienced reporter dig up if he was curious enough?'

'You've been coming here—each day—to investigate *me*?' Despite all the evidence laid out in front of her, Louisa was still struggling to believe any of this. 'For what purpose, for goodness' sake?'

'For the purpose of being prepared for the enterprising person who decides to drag my name through the mud if or when it comes to light that Max Landreau's long-term live-in mistress is also my wife.'

As if he'd slapped her face, Louisa drew in a sharp breath. 'I am not Max's mistress.'

'His long-term live-in—what, then?'

'Assistant,' she insisted. 'His *personal* assistant. My duties deal with the *personal* and *social* side of his life but I *don't* sleep with him.'

'Intriguing,' he drawled, turning to settle his lean hips against the desk again with that same long, relaxed sprawl of his legs. 'You live in his house—'

'I do not!' she denied. 'I rent the flat above his garages!'

'You *live* in his house,' he repeated. 'It is your *permanent* address. You have a *permanent* stateroom on his yacht! Wherever he goes you go as if joined to him at the hip!'

His voice had hardened and thickened with each declaration he'd tossed at her. Reaching round, he snatched up the folder and in a shocking display of uncharacteristic carelessness sent a spill of papers sliding onto the desk as he flipped through them with long fingers to filter out several computer-generated photographs.

'You,' he said, 'in a hot-pink bikini, leaning against him at a lunch party on his yacht.' He showed her. 'You,' he continued, 'wearing the slinkiest red dress I have ever seen, pinned to his side by the diamonds you wear around your beautiful throat at a charity ball at his house! Then we have the beach party in the south of France, where you use him as a pillow while he shades your face from the sun with his hat. You are laughing!' he accused, as if laughing was a very big sin in his eyes. 'You are wearing a white bikini! He wears nothing!'

'Sh-shorts,' Louisa stammered, face going pinker with each revealing photograph. 'Max has sh-shorts on.'

'He does not wear his shorts up as high as that muscle bronzed chest you are so comfortable with!'

She gasped as he flung the images at her. They fell in a slithering waft to the floor while he launched himself away from the desk. Shaken by his sudden burst of violence, Louisa just stared after him, not sure what to say in her own defence. She *did* travel wherever Max travelled. She did *live-in*, if that phrase could still be innocent after the rude interpretation Andreas had put on it. And the pictures did look pretty intimate, she allowed reluctantly.

'I don't sleep with him,' she insisted.

'Who mentioned sleep?' he spun to rake back. He was vibrating with anger now, riding on a river of it. 'The guy romantically *proposed* to you on top of the London Eye in front of a thousand guests—I watched the replay on the internet!'

The way his fingers shook as he scraped them through his hair almost made Louisa feel sorry for him—if he hadn't roughed out a very rude word that stiffened her spine on an offended jolt.

'It was six guests, and it was a publicity stunt,' she corrected, refusing to admit how angry she'd been with Max for pulling the silly stunt at all. 'He works in the media! He lives a very high-profile life!'

'With my wife as his sexy little sidekick—am I supposed to be pleased to see you with him like that?'

'How come you didn't see the London Eye thing when it happened?' she retaliated hotly. 'It went worldwide at the time, so what were *you* doing in June last year while I was being proposed to, Andreas—hiding away in your *island retreat* with one of your floozies?'

'Did you want me to see you?'

The challenge locked her eyes on his face, her mouth dropping open on a gasping quiver of shock.

'Tall, dark, handsome media mogul, older than me but not by much, filthy rich,' he listed, using each word like a punch. 'Have you been using him as a substitute for me because you missed me, *agape mou*... have you spent the last four years waiting for me to notice you with him so I would come and claim you back?'

CHAPTER ELEVEN

'YOU conceited devil,' Louisa whispered.

But could what he said be true? Had she been using her working relationship with Max as a safe substitute for the man she loved—had she unconsciously *wanted* Andreas to see her happy with Max?

Unconsciously done or not, the mere idea devastated her, it glazed her blue eyes and whirled her into a cold, dark, empty place of hopeless self-deceit. If that was what she'd been doing, she might as well have turned to drugs and hidden from herself that way. She might as well have stayed hysterical and let them lock her away in a padded cell because this was worse—these years of hidden pining were oh, so much worse!

'Well, I am here now, so you can forget about Landreau.'

Louisa blinked, slow to open her eyes again on this horrible new view of herself he was making her face. When she did manage it she found that Andreas had moved closer; in fact, he was standing right over her with his glinting dark gaze fixed on her pale, too expressive face.

'You think you are better than him,' she realised shakily.

'I know I am better than him,' he responded arrogantly.

'Within hours of us meeting again you were all over me as if we had never been parted.' Reaching out, he brushed a silken strand of freshly washed hair behind her ear in that achingly familiar tender gesture she'd always read as a form of apology—this time it felt like an act of contempt. 'Whatever he did for you, it was no substitute for the real thing, was it? One kiss in the dark in a dusty car park and you were mine again.'

He said that as if it were a foregone conclusion. Well, it wasn't! Shuddering, she reached up to knock his hand away. 'If you're this sure of me, then why go after Max at all?' she challenged, indicating Max's life spread out on his desk.

'Insurance,' he said. 'He might decide to come chasing after you and you might decide to be stubborn and continue to lie to yourself as well as to him. How did you find out what I've been doing here?' he then asked curiously.

Pressing her lips together, Louisa folded her arms around her body then told him about Max's phone call.

'Good, he's panicking,' Andreas declared in flat satisfaction. 'He might have a lot going for him but he knows I can bring him crashing within twenty-four hours if I so wished.'

He was that sure of himself, Louisa noted bitterly—*that* powerful now? The knowledge shook her. 'But you don't wish to, do you?' She lifted her head to watch a grimace twist the ruthless line of his mouth.

'I want my wife back without the risk of a scandal.'

And there was the threat, she heard. She played it his way or else Max paid the price. How could she have let herself forget his vengeful desire to make others pay for their interference in their lives—for their lost five years? His family, her family…now Max had been added to the list.

This wasn't about the two of them recapturing what they had used to have, it was about Andreas winning. It was a cold, cold moment when Louisa looked at him and finally accepted how much he had changed. His father must be proud of him; his son had grown tougher and more ruthless than the great Orestes himself.

'All this work you've done is for nothing,' she heard herself murmur in a shaky voice as bitter as the truth she had just been made to face. 'You see, you picked the wrong fight, because I am not coming back to you.'

With that she pushed past him.

'You are choosing him over me? This is mad.' His hand caught her back. 'Do you think your substitute lover will take you back now that I have him hanging by his fingernails? You should have told him who you really belong to, Louisa.'

Louisa swung round. 'Max has always known about you,' she fired back furiously. 'And we have never been lovers!' she all but screeched.

'Four years in his constant company? Of course you slept with him!' he dished out with yet more of that hurtful contempt. 'Why can't you just be honest with me about it?'

Honest? She tugged her wrist free. 'Can *you* stand right here in front of me, Andreas, and *honestly* state that you have never taken another woman to your bed?'

The air grew thick with his pulsing stillness, the skin covering his face went tight. Shaking, simmering, refusing to let go of his diamond-hard eyes, Louisa waited for his answer while it throbbed and prickled and rattled around inside her because—

'You know you cannot,' she finally said for him.

'Especially when I saw you with my own eyes, shacked up with that woman in *our* apartment in Athens, in *our* bed!'

He went so pale Louisa thought he was going to keel over—in fact, she wished that he would!

'No,' he denied. 'You could not—'

'Now who's hiding the truth?' she laughed, spinning away from him, only to spin right back to add bitterly, 'I have told you once already that I knew about her,' though he'd so conveniently forgotten that she'd said it at all! 'I came back here to the villa to *you*, but the only people here were Kostas and your dear brother Alex.' She had to stop to draw in a thick breath. 'Alex told me you were living in Athens, that you had not been back to the island at all! So I asked him to arrange me a flight. He warned me not to bother. I was history, he said. You'd moved on! I refused to listen to his poison and insisted he arrange me a helicopter, but I should have listened to him, shouldn't I, Andreas, because this time his warning was genuine!'

He'd gone paler with each ugly word she'd thrown at him. 'When?' he demanded roughly, '*When* did this happen?'

'Six weeks after I'd left here.' Turning away because she could no longer look at him, Louisa wrapped her arms around her shivering body and felt her fingernails bite into her flesh. 'I went straight to the apartment. I let myself in with my key. The signs of your habitation were everywhere. It—it looked like you'd been enjoying one heck of a good party!'

His thick curse raked across her flesh.

'I see you've remembered which day it is I am talking about,' she swung back to slice at him, 'unless, of course, you had been enjoying wild parties there every night after you walked out and left me alone here!'

It was his turn to swing his back to her and he said absolutely nothing. He just pushed a hand up to grip the back of his neck, making muscles bunch all over him, his amazing damn shoulders racked up tight.

'I left as quietly as I'd arrived,' she continued with effort. 'I didn't think a forgotten wife singing out "Hi, I'm back!" would have done much for the—pleasures you were in the process of sleeping off.'

'You can stop now,' he roughed out. 'I know what you saw.'

'Good.' So why did it hurt so badly that he wasn't making excuses? Why couldn't he just come up with some clever quick *lie* to explain away what she'd seen? And why did she want him to?

The answer was so deeply humiliating it made her cringe inside her own flesh. Hot dry tears burned the back of her throat and she knew she just had to get out of here.

Shaking, Louisa turned to head for the door.

'Where are you going?' he ground out.

'I would have thought it was obvious. I'm leaving.'

'To go back to Landreau?' The hard cynicism in his voice cut her to the raw.

Her narrow back tensed inside the blue sundress, hair sliding down her back as her chin shot up with a jerk. Barely able to breathe across the ice suddenly flowing through her veins, Louisa turned to look at him—look at her tall, dark, handsome husband who had about as much faith in her word as she'd ever had in this crazy second chance of their marriage working out.

He was looking at her now, angry—contemptuous. 'Well, don't kid yourself that you are the only woman he sleeps with. There is at least one other woman out there who shares his bed when you are not in it,' he extended brutally. 'Can you live with that?'

'And how many lovers have passed through your bed, Andreas?' she flung right back. 'One or two, a dozen—a hundred—?'

His mouth took on that grim flat line in refusal to answer and he went to turn away again. On a blazing flare of anger Louisa walked back to him and grabbed hold of his arm to swing him back. 'You demanded honesty between us, so answer the question!'

'So fierce.' He laughed oddly.

'Tell me!'

'Have I taken other women to my bed?' suddenly he was all sardonic arrogance. 'Of course,' he responded. 'Five years is a long time to spend celibate.'

She let go of his arm as if it repelled her, inside she was a shivering, quivering wreck of hurt and disgust. 'So the old Greek double standard is still alive and kicking,' she breathed acidly. 'I hope you enjoy living up to it.'

With that she walked back to the door on legs that felt as unstable as the tears she was fighting.

'What is that supposed to mean?' he roughed out.

'You said it first—five years apart?' Fingers taking a white-knuckled grip on the door handle, she sent him a deriding look. 'You don't really think that *I* haven't been playing the field like you *and* Max, do you…?'

She watched him tense, watched his beautiful bronzed skin whiten, watched him turn himself into a block of stone. That she could also see he actually believed what she was saying sent the death rattle of her love for him rolling through her heart and across her throat.

'If I'm pregnant I'll let you know—if you're still interested by then,' was her final cold volley before she walked out.

Kostas and Pietros were nowhere to be seen, which suited her fine because she didn't want to see anyone. She just wanted to get away from here and never come back.

Isabella was about to get her dearest wish, she thought bitterly as she stepped down from the shady veranda into the fierce midday heat.

Tugging in a thick breath of air, she set off walking down the long driveway without a single clue as to where she was going to go. The other house was out of the question, she even shuddered at the idea of going back there. The hotel was out too, since there was no way she was going to be able to put on a nice, polite face for everyone there.

Which left only one other place for her to go and it drew her like a homing pigeon, keeping her moving down the long driveway, and she was not—not—*not* going to cry! she told herself.

The angry roar of a car engine coming up fast from behind stiffened her backbone. Her chin shot up, eyes hot and dry, mouth quivering, her insides heaving and twisting with the multitude of emotions playing havoc with her as she quickened her pace.

The open-top car came to a screeching stop beside her. 'Get in,' Andreas commanded harshly.

Louisa just kept on walking. There was a curse and a click then he was out of the car and around the bonnet and blocking her path before she could manage to draw breath.

'Get in the car, Louisa, if you don't want me to pick you up and *put* you in!' he rasped out angrily.

She heaved in a deep breath. 'I don't—'

He picked her up and dumped her in the car seat right over the top of the door. The sheer shock of it stung through her in a trembling fizz that chased up and down her limbs.

She was still trembling when he got in beside her and threw the car into gear then shot off down the drive. 'You are going to have to stop walking away from me,' he growled roughly.

'*Me* walk away from *you*?' Shaken up, hair flying as she swung her flashing blue eyes up to glare at his face, only to have her heart dance off in a skittering flurry when she found herself staring at an Andreas she had never seen before.

His lean golden profile stood right on the cutting edge of murder—tense and tight, the steel-rimmed sunglasses covering his eyes filling her head with fantastical images of hard, handsome hit men of the coldly ruthless kind. Something else sprang to life inside her and sizzled, making her look away again quickly, not happy at all to feel the full impact of his attraction in such a way.

'We *both* have to stop walking away from each other, then,' he amended tightly. 'Whatever. It stops right here!'

Hot tears were beginning to take her over, she watched them blur out her vision. 'So we can flog this marriage to death some more?'

With a jerk, he pulled the car to a stop at the junction with the road to let an ancient truck pass by. It struggled on the slight incline, belching out diesel fumes and its old engine growling like a great angry mammoth.

'It isn't dead yet.'

It was in Louisa's opinion! 'I don't want to stay married to a man who can't even trust me when I tell him the truth,' she said, conveniently forgetting the lie she had tossed at him just before she'd left.

The old truck rolled past. Andreas made no answer, just eased his foot off the brake in the wake of the lorry's lumbering upheaval and swung them out onto the road.

'You're going the wrong way again,' she told him thickly. 'I was going to visit Nikos.'

A muscle flicked in his taut jaw, other muscles clenching elsewhere at the same time as he gave the engine more speed. Barely thirty seconds later and he was slowing down again to swing the car onto a narrow track that would take them up the hill behind the luxury villas. Instant recognition as to what exactly lay on the other side of that hill made Louisa tense in her seat.

'No,' she gasped out. 'Andreas, you can't do this!'

He turned to look at her through those steel-rimmed sunglasses. 'When are you going to recognise that I can do very much as I please?'

The coolly delivered statement left Louisa gasping. True alarm caused a whole new set of senses to spring into life inside her, most of them circling around the knowledge that he hadn't just said that to score points.

He was different. From the moment she'd stepped into that hi-tech study in the family villa she'd been looking at and dealing with a completely different man from the one he had let her see while they'd been living in that crazy bubble they'd created around themselves at the other house. Now the bubble had burst it was like dealing with a stranger, a stranger hell-bent on doing what he wished.

'But I w-want to visit Nikos.' It broke from her in a tearful, pained plea.

It was as if she'd stuck pins in him the way his muscles flinched, but it didn't stop him driving them over the peak of the hill. A moment later he turned them off the track and drove through a pair of security gates that swung open by some invisible command.

Louisa found herself staring at the Markonos private heliport complete with hangar tucked neatly into the bowl of the hill. A shiny white helicopter stood idle on the concrete helipad. As they shot to a halt beside it she could see a pilot already ensconced in the cockpit, and over by the hangar several employees were loitering, awaiting their arrival.

'Wh-when did you arrange all of this?' she breathed unsteadily.

'Before I came after you.'

With a long-limbed, lithe grace he climbed out of the car, leaving her sitting there coming to terms with this new view of him. He came round the car and opened her door for her then bent to unfasten her seat belt. An engine started up, rotor blades whirred into life.

'I'm not getting on that,' she refused as he drew her to her feet.

He turned to toss the car keys at one of the loitering men. His hand still manacled her wrist. She gave a tug to get free but, like the last time, his fingers tightened. He was playing it tough again, he was playing it ruthless, only this time it wasn't just a half-empty house on the island he was dragging her off to, it was a helicopter that could be taking her anywhere!

'Will you listen to me?' Desperation made her swing round so she was standing in front of him, and pure compulsion made her reach up and snatch the sunglasses from his face. She found herself staring up at his hard, tight, lean golden features with glinting black eyes that offered no hope of a compromise.

'Y-you're delusional if you think I'm just meekly going to board that thing without you explaining why the heck I should!' Desperately she tried to grab back some control here.

'Delusional?' he repeated. 'Well, let us see about that, shall we?'

She saw what was coming. Her breathing feathered. She put both hands to his chest as if to ward him off but the flashing burn in his eyes told her that nothing was going to stop him as he lowered his head and claimed her mouth. The hot sting of desire leapt to life in her bloodstream and her helpless groan vibrated across each separate layer of her skin. He possessed her mouth—all of it. He threw everything into that kiss, every bit of angrily passionate frustration he was feeling. He kissed her until her legs couldn't support her, until her fingers crushed his glasses into her palm and her other hand crawled up his chest to cling around his neck. He used his hands to keep her pressed up against his body and let her feel what was happening to him. And he did it knowingly, ruthlessly, until her mouth throbbed and her blood pounded and her thighs pulsed and danced.

And he did it right there in full view of his watching pilot and the ground staff. When he lifted his head he waited in silence until she opened her kiss-drugged, man-possessed eyes.

'Was that real enough?' he asked then.

'Yes,' was the only breathless little answer she had to give him.

'Sure you don't want to argue the point some more?'

Pressing her pulsing lips together, she shook her head.

'Then do you walk onto the helicopter or do I carry you there too?'

'W-walk,' she whispered.

He nodded, then, because she looked so beaten, he sighed and said roughly, 'Don't look so hopeless. You know I will never harm a single golden hair on your beautiful head.'

Strangely she did know; in fact, it was the only comfort she had to cling to as she let him walk her onto that helicopter without kicking up a screaming fuss.

The Markonos fleet of executive helicopters were not what you could ever call standard issue. The rich cream leather and glossy walnut veneer interior made yet another statement of wealth and of power she had conveniently let herself forget.

'Jamie,' she remembered as he saw her settled into one of the seats.

'Your brother is being well cared for,' he assured her.

'What is that supposed to mean?' she asked warily, something in the cool way he had said it making her frown.

He took a mobile phone out of his trouser pocket. 'Jamie has been watched over by one of my people since I agreed to let him stay at the hotel instead of moving into the villa with us.'

'Your people? Do you mean like the man you instructed to watch my every movement when you *walked away* earlier this week?'

The tart stab made his firm mouth flex. 'I look after my own,' was all he said.

Then he dropped the mobile phone on her lap and took back the sunglasses she had forgotten she was holding. 'You have three minutes to assure your brother that everything is fine between us,' he instructed as he turned away from her. 'You can tell him we are on our way to Athens and will be back on the island before nightfall—'

'Athens? I don't want to go to…'

Louisa found herself protesting to a walnut-veneered bulkhead. He'd just walked through the door and into the pilot's cabin without giving her a chance to finish what she'd been going to say! Sitting back in her seat, she picked up the mobile. By the time she'd finished assuring her brother that everything was absolutely fine, they were lifting off the ground.

CHAPTER TWELVE

SHE didn't see Andreas again until they landed at a private airstrip in Athens, which gave her more than long enough to list every nasty, sneaky thing he had done, so she was wound up like a spring-loaded clock by the time he reappeared to escort her into the waiting limousine.

A chauffeur-driven limousine with no central partition to give her the privacy she needed to say what she wanted to say—not that a partition would have made much difference because Andreas, she discovered, was quite capable of putting up his own partition.

So the air simmered between them as they drove into Athens and the closer they got to the luxury houses and apartment blocks of Kolaniki the more uptight she became.

'I don't want to visit your parents,' she bit out when that horror scenario flicked into her head.

He said nothing, his closed profile making her fingers itch so badly to slap him into a reaction that she had to curl them into fists on her lap.

What was he up to—what was he thinking?

Andreas knew exactly what he was up to but the hell if he was going to let her know it—he wasn't that brave. His throat tightened when he tried to swallow as they bypassed the road leading to the luxury houses that dotted Kolaniki Hill with its famous views over Athens and he felt her stiffen in the seat beside him. He was taking such a big risk here he wasn't that certain he could carry it through.

'I hate you,' she whispered when they pulled into the fore-court of his apartment block. She was white as a sheet now, eyes too big and too dark in the pinched strain of her face. 'I don't know how you can bring yourself to do this to me.'

The chauffeur climbed out of the car.

'Try cutting me a bit of slack, *agape mou*,' Andreas returned huskily. 'I need to do this. We need to do it.'

Need to do what, though? Break her heart all over again?

The chauffeur opened her door for her, giving her little option but to step out of the car's air-conditioned interior into the full humid weight of the afternoon heat.

It had taken barely an hour to get here, barely an hour to repeat a trip she had last made five years before. Now her heart was flailing around in her stomach. Any second now she knew she was going to be sick.

Andreas climbed out on the other side of the car and gave a nod at the chauffeur, who disappeared back inside the car and drove it away around the side of the building to where the garages were situated, leaving the two of them staring at each other across the empty gap.

He looked big, lean, tough—determined. Having got her this far with his grim bullying tactics, Louisa didn't doubt she would find herself yanked over his shoulder in a fireman's lift if she did not let him finish whatever it was he was so hell-bent on doing here.

So she made herself cross the gap separating them,

chin up, blue eyes so cold they even felt like chips of ice. As she continued past him into the building's elegant foyer the flat of his hand arrived, warm against the base of her spine.

Yet another statement of possession, she noted with a stinging tensing of her body as she flinched right away from him. She didn't want him to touch her—she didn't want to be here at all.

They stepped into the waiting lift like two separate entities and rode up to the top floor without saying a word. He did not take his darkly hooded eyes from her face, while she stared at the floor and hoped to God she could get through this without throwing up.

The lift opened directly into the apartment with its open-plan luxury that looked exactly the same as it had done five years ago, only without the evidence of partying to litter it up. It still bore the same classic modern furniture that had *man* stamped all over it because Andreas had owned this apartment long before she had come into his life.

The lift door swished shut, she couldn't hold back a cold shiver, and her arms flung themselves around her body as if doing so would ward off what was throbbing away inside her trying to get out.

But still he hadn't finished with this torture, coming to place that hand back on her spine, he ignored her stiffened rejection of it this time and made the hand a stubborn arm which propelled her across the living room to a door that, she recalled to her sinking horror, led through to the other rooms in this vast and elegantly sprawling place.

'Don't…' she couldn't stop herself from quivering out when he stopped outside the door to their old bedroom.

Still keeping her trapped by that controlling arm, he flung the door open and urged her inside. For the next thirty seconds she just stopped functioning, her knees went hollow, her throat closing up. Everything was the same in here—everything, right down to the huge bed with its snowy white linen she only had to take a fleeting glance at to need to push a hand up to cover her mouth. Once again the only things missing were the littered signs of occupation.

'The last time you came here I would have willingly died rather than let you see what you did,' his voice came deep and gruff from behind her, 'but I was out of it, beyond the point of being any use to anyone, including a wife who deserved to find a man waiting here for her, not a stoned-out-of-his-head wimp.'

Well, he said it, Louisa thought starkly, pressing her fingers up to her lips, only to feel them tremble against her chattering teeth.

'I want to beg your forgiveness.'

Right here at the scene of his crime? 'Not a good venue for begging me for anything,' she whispered.

'An explanation, then,' he persisted tautly. 'Will you accept an explanation?'

Oh, God, did she have to? 'Look,' she spun round, aiming her hurt gaze at a point somewhere between his tense left shoulder and the door, 'y-you don't need to do this. I had already accepted wh-what I'd seen here or I would not have let you—'

'Stop lying to me,' he ground out.

She knew her face was white because it *felt* white! She knew her lips were trembling and her heart was pounding and— 'I don't *need* you to do this, Andreas! I don't want you to do this! I just w-want to get out of here—'

'Well, I *need* to do this!' He reached out to catch hold of her shoulders, two tense hands gripping her as if they wanted to give her a damn good shake. 'It cannot hurt you to listen,' he said roughly.

No? 'Confession might be good for your soul but it does absolutely nothing for mine!'

'*I love you!*' he raked out. 'I have *always* loved you! I never *stopped* loving you. I don't *want* to stop loving you! Does that make your soul feel good?'

With a rasping sigh he let go of her, pacing away across the room like a man who regretted saying all of that now it was out and it was too late.

Totally silenced, Louisa stared after him, watching as he lifted a clenched fist as if to send it grinding into the wall in front of him—then he changed his mind and turned.

'Do you remember Lilia?' he asked huskily.

Lilia? Louisa found she couldn't remember anything. 'You love me?' It came out in a thick, breathless jerk.

'Yes,' he hissed. 'Do you remember her?'

Lilia…Y-your cousin?' She nodded, managing to pull up an image of a beautiful creature with gorgeous dark eyes and a fabulous figure. 'Why didn't you say sooner— a-about loving me?'

'Because I was waiting for you to say it first,' His mouth twisted into a grimace that he turned into a sigh. 'It was Lilia you saw me with.'

'You went to bed with your cousin Lilia?' The shock and the horror of it almost knocked Louisa off her feet.

'What do you take me for?' He tensed up angrily.

'A drunk?' she suggested wildly. 'Y-you went to bed with your cousin Lilia because you were drunk, and you think this kind of confession is good for your soul?'

'I did not go to bed with her!' He sighed. 'Why don't you just shut up and listen to what I have to say?'

It was all she could do to get her shaky legs to carry her the couple of steps needed to sink down on the nearest chair. Listening at this moment was very much beyond her while she was trying to recall what she had seen that day.

But all that would come to mind was Andreas lying there on that bed, naked from what she could tell by the way the sheet rode low on his hips, while his beautiful companion lay beside him apparently wrapped in what was left of the sheet. She'd had a naked arm curved around his shoulders, and her face had been pushed up close to his sleeping face with the long mane of her glossy black hair tumbling out behind her over the pillow.

'Lilia rescued me from drowning in a sea of booze and self-pity,' his deep voice impinged, making her blink into focus on him. He'd moved again and was leaning against the wall now, with his fists shoved out of sight in his trouser pockets, his expression oddly rueful even while it was tense.

'I came back from trying to see you in England and locked myself away in here with a crate of whisky and no desire to see anyone,' he went on. 'I switched off my mobile and unplugged the phone. I hated myself. I hated you. I had sunk so low I was quite content to waste away right here in this apartment, and I would have done it if Lilia had not turned up and bullied the janitor to let her in. She was tough…'

A hard-crusted businesswoman who'd inherited her

father's stake in the Markonos empire and had been determined to hold on to her share of power, Louisa recalled.

'She found me sprawled on the bed fully clothed and out cold with a bottle of whisky still clutched in my fingers. She shook me awake and generally shouted and bullied me until I agreed to get up and take a shower. I was a mess,' he admitted. 'I couldn't even walk straight, never mind stand upright, so Lilia did it. She all but carried me into the shower then got in there with me—stripped my clothes off and somehow managed to keep me propped against the wall until the freezing cold water started to sober me up. Then she pulled me out of the shower and told me to dry myself and get a shave while she took one of the towels and went back into the bedroom to get out of her wet clothes. I cut myself,' he recalled, lifting a hand out of his pocket to touch his jaw as if the cut were still there. 'By the time I put in an appearance in the bedroom she was wearing the towel and had stripped the bed and was smoothing out the clean sheet...'

He stopped speaking for a moment, the hand lowering back into his pocket, then he gave a shake of his head.

'I still don't understand why it happened,' he continued huskily. 'I mean, you are so fair and Lilia is so dark, but—when she glanced up and smiled at me, that smile reminded me so much of you that I just...fell apart. I sobbed like a baby.' He roughed out the confession. 'I cried for you, I cried for myself, I cried for Nikos...'

Unable to just sit there when she could see he was struggling, Louisa got up and went to slide her arms around him. 'You don't have to say any more,' she whispered painfully. 'I know how you felt,' because she'd been there, oh, she'd been there...

But Andreas didn't want to stop. 'Once I let the floodgates open I could do nothing to close them again. Lilia somehow managed to get me to the bed, though the hell knows how she managed it. Then she lay down beside me and held me. She just held me while the storm raged until eventually we both must have fallen into an exhausted sleep.'

'I wish I'd had a Lilia,' Louisa murmured. 'Instead I got panicked parents who called the doctor and had me taken away.'

'I wish I had been there to be your Lilia.' His arms came around her, strong and tense. 'We could have poured it all out together as it should have been, and the last five years of hell would not have happened.'

His tone had toughened. Louisa looked at him anxiously. 'Don't go down the revenge track again,' she begged.

'I'm not.' He shook his head. 'It might have taken me a few minutes longer than it should, but when you walked out on me at the villa it suddenly hit me that I had been fighting the wrong battles all along. Landreau did not matter, our two meddling families did not matter. Even the fabulous sex we've been indulging in did not matter, it was the fact that you could still let me love you like that, believing what you believed you saw here. That was my real victory, though I was in danger of letting it slip through my fingers.'

'Hence the kidnap.' Louisa was impressed by his recovery tactics.

He pushed his hand through her hair, his dark eyes remaining sombre as he released a sigh. 'I don't care about your other lovers, *agape mou*,' he murmured. 'I did not deserve that you could let *me* come near you again, so how can I resent them?'

'Because you're Greek, with unforgivable double standards?' Louisa suggested.

He grimaced.

'Because you're arrogant and pushy and conceited,' she added, 'and can't tell the difference between the truth and a lie when it's stabbed at you with the intent to draw blood?'

He frowned.

It was Louisa's turn to let her soft mouth twist out a grimace. 'There haven't been any other men, Andreas—and that includes Max,' she took pains to impress.

Andreas pulled in a deep breath then let it out again. 'I definitely did not deserve to hear you say that.'

'So you're going to believe me this time?'

He smiled ruefully. 'Yes, please.'

'I fell for you when I was seventeen and I haven't wanted another man since,' she confided. 'You were right when you said I'd used my relationship with Max to hide behind. Perhaps I even used it to make—*hope* to make you come and claim me back, I'm still not quite ready to admit that one to myself.'

'And I definitely did not deserve to hear you say that,' Andreas impressed.

Louisa nodded in agreement, her gaze and her attention now fixed on his mouth because it had relaxed at last, looking more like the sexy mouth she so loved to—

'Especially not when I haven't finished my own confessions yet…' that beautiful mouth wryly tagged on.

Louisa didn't want to hear any more right now, she just wanted to—

'About my other women…'

'No.' Her spine arched as she drew back from him. 'Trust me when I say I don't want to hear about them.'

'No, trust me that you will want to hear it when I tell you that nothing happened with them.'

She was slow to lift her eyes to his because he had to be just saying that to make her feel better. 'It's the truth,' he said softly. 'They were not you. They made great arm candy but I didn't want them for anything else. They were too proud to admit to anyone that I did *not* take them to bed, so my reputation as this fabulous lover grew from their face-saving lies.'

'Andreas, I never expected you to remain faithful to me after we split up,' and Louisa knew him. Five days was a long time for him to go without indulging his very healthy sex drive, never mind five years!

He laughed, a thick sound that seemed to mock himself. 'Why do you think I fell on you like a sex-starved lunatic up on the hill?' he asked. 'Why do you think I acted like a great, hungry bear with no damn finesse? You,' he said when she looked up at him. 'I had *you* back in my arms and my libido went from nil to rampant…'

Oh, my, Louisa thought, her eyes darkening because she was starting to believe him—had to do when she saw the expression on his face. 'You're serious,' she laughed.

'A man does not lay out his failings to have them laughed at,' he protested.

'I'm not laughing.' Louisa moved in closer. 'I'm really very impressed.'

'So you should be.' He was regretting the confession now, she could tell by the frown grabbing at his eyebrows.

'So what happens next?' she murmured, wanting to kiss

him, wanting to drag his clothes off him so badly she ought to be ashamed at how wanton she felt—but she wasn't.

He read the look in her eyes and pushed out a heavy breath. 'What the hell do you think happens next?' He caught her up off her feet. 'We are going to build new good memories over the top of your bad memories in this bed.'

Louisa sighed as he tumbled her down on the soft mattress. 'I love it when you come over all masterful and primitive,' she confided.

EPILOGUE

ANDREAS was lazing out on the sun deck beneath the shade of a huge umbrella, with his three-month-old daughter lying curled up and fast asleep on his chest. The strong-muscled arm he had curving around that fragile little body went so perfectly with the contented expression on his handsome face.

'Well, what do you think?' Louisa asked the small male version she had cradled in her arms. 'Do we wake them up or leave them to it?'

'I am awake,' Andreas's sleepily husky voice murmured. 'Where have you been all of this time?'

'I've been answering a million phone calls from family,' she answered drily.

He was slow to open his eyes and the cynical look she saw glinting in them made Louisa grimace. 'So they are all falling over themselves to make their peace?'

'Better that than letting you line them up to shoot them,' she responded.

'I have no wish to shoot them any more,' he denied. 'I just did not want them intruding on our lives again, that's all.'

'Well, they're all coming to celebrate the twins' name-day,' Louisa said firmly, 'and you are going to behave yourself.'

Scooping his daughter into the crook of his arm, Andreas dropped a gentle kiss on her tiny button nose then sat up, bronzed muscles rippling in a way that shot a familiar injection of heat into Louisa's too susceptible abdomen.

'That depends on the incentives on offer,' he drawled.

'Good food,' she said, 'a packed chapel and a great party afterwards?'

'Not enough.' Coming to his feet wearing only a pair of sexy shorts, he stepped over to her to look down at his peacefully sleeping son, made that tiny nose twitch when he dropped a kiss on it too, then looked up straight into Louisa's eyes.

'You want an afternoon of rampant sex while these two sleep,' she read in that look.

Andreas gave a shake of his head. 'I get that by demand without having to put up with family.'

'Then what do you want?'

'Another set of these,' he answered coolly.

Louisa let loose with a choked laugh that disturbed both sleeping babies. 'You must be joking! I've only just got over having Tabatha and Leon!'

'But it took a whole year to conceive them,' Andreas pointed out. 'So the way I see it, if we start now, by the time their next name-day comes along I might not even need an incentive to put up with family...'

Two years and he still had not come to forgive them for messing with their lives. Two years, two babies...Louisa sighed as she walked into the house so beautifully finished now with a soft, warm homeliness about it she just loved.

They each bent over a white cot to place a baby down. Then like homing pigeons they both straightened and walked over to the cedar-wood dresser on which stood the framed picture of Nikos, surrounded by a collection of little toy cars.

'Nikos would love us to have a large family,' Andreas said as a set of his long fingers reached out to gently straighten the cars.

'That was such a low-down, blatant attempt to tug at my heartstrings,' Louisa complained as she kissed her fingertips then placed them on her eldest son's smiling cherub mouth.

Andreas just shrugged and followed her as she walked out of the nursery. 'Don't forget we are still playing five years of catch-up.'

'Not with my body, we're not.'

His hands arrived at her hips to draw her against him as they entered their bedroom. 'Just think,' he said softly, 'of all those afternoons and nights of wild sex with no protection.'

The contraceptive pill didn't suit her, which meant that Andreas had to use something. Both of them hated it.

As he moved his fingers to the clasp of her shorts, his teeth arrived at her nape. 'I'll let you crawl all over me to your heart's content and I won't even complain when you make me beg.'

A long-fingered hand slipped into her loosened shorts and that fabulous sting of anticipation filtered like a magic potion through Louisa's blood. She quivered as he touched her. He growled out a sound of satisfaction because he could bring her alive with nothing much.

'And if you happen to be one-hit potent this time?' she managed to gasp out. 'I'll be pregnant and fat with a baby stuck on each hip. Where is the incentive for me in being put through that?'

'I will throw in a houseful of nannies.' He caught her shivered gasp in his mouth as his stroking touch went more intimate. 'I will cut down my travelling—give it all to Alex.'

'You already do that,' she quivered out.

'He's surprisingly good at it.' The rueful tone accompanied the complete removal of her shorts as they dropped to her feet.

One day she would pay attention as to how he managed to strip himself naked while toying with her like this but for now…she turned to look at him, all heavy-eyed, sensual woman hungry for her man.

'This was supposed to be a discussion about your objection to family, not about me giving you more babies,' she reminded him.

He caught hold of the edges of her T-shirt and stripped it off over her head. 'I adore my family,' he murmured as his hand caught the swing of her breasts and his mouth captured her lips. 'This family,' he added, edging her backwards towards the bed. 'I might learn to tolerate the others if you give me what I want.'

'Lots of sex with no protection?' Louisa asked for confirmation as he tumbled her onto the bed.

'I am Greek, we love big families. We love our wives pregnant and fat. And just think of all that loving from your man with no protection to spoil it,' he urged as he came to lie over her. 'I can make you feel so wonderful you will never want to get out of this bed…'

He was not short on arrogance or conceit, Louisa mused hazily as he took her away and right out of herself. In the two years since the big scene in their apartment in Athens, she had come to know the two sides of Andreas Markonos, and *both* were sensationally irresistible. The guy in the sharp suit with his tycoon head on could take her breath away with just a fleeting glance. The guy wearing shorts was the one she'd met ten years ago and he still had the power to turn her inside out.

She loved them both. She adored them both. When his name appeared in the media these days she swelled with pride at whatever big deal he had managed to pull off against all the odds, and couldn't wait for him to come home so she could take his tycoon clothes off. When they went out together she adored the way he kept her at his side—joined at the hip, as he liked to describe it. She loved the hungry, possessive way he looked at her when she was all dressed up and the way he glowered when she sparkled for other men.

And she absolutely totally and forever loved it when he did this to her. By the time it was over and as usual, she had lost the will to even breathe.

'You did that without my say-so,' she complained but without any substance to give it punch.

'You loved it,' he assured arrogantly as he lay heavy on her.

'Mm,' she agreed then opened her eyes to look at him. 'I love you so much,' she whispered. 'Don't ever stop loving me and wanting me like this.'

'As if,' he smiled and started kissing her again.

* * * * *

THOROUGHBRED LEGACY
*The stakes are high when it comes to love,
horse racing, family secrets
and broken promises.*

*A new exciting Harlequin continuity series coming soon!
Led by* New York Times *bestselling author
Elizabeth Bevarly*
FLIRTING WITH TROUBLE

Here's a preview

THE DOOR CLOSED behind them, throwing them into darkness and leaving them utterly alone. And the next thing Daniel knew, he heard himself saying, "Marnie, I'm sorry about the way things turned out in Del Mar."

She said nothing at first, only strode across the room and stared out the window beside him. Although he couldn't see her well in the darkness—he still hadn't switched on a light…but then, neither had she—he imagined her expression was a little preoccupied, a little anxious, a little confused.

Finally, very softly, she said, "Are you?"

He nodded, then, worried she wouldn't be able to see the gesture, added, "Yeah. I am. I should have said good-bye to you."

"Yes, you should have."

Actually, he thought, there were a lot of things he should have done in Del Mar. He'd had *a lot* riding on the Pacific Classic, and even more on his entry, Little Joe, but after meeting Marnie, the Pacific Classic had been the last thing on Daniel's mind. His loss at Del Mar had pretty much ended his career before it had even begun, and he'd had to start all over again, rebuilding from nothing.

He simply had not then and did not now have room in his life for a woman as potent as Marnie Roberts. He was a horseman first and foremost. From the time he was a schoolboy, he'd known what he wanted to do with his life—be the best possible trainer he could be.

He had to make sure Marnie understood—and he understood, too—why things had ended the way they had eight years ago. He just wished he could find the words to do that. Hell, he wished he could find the *thoughts* to do that.

"You made me forget things, Marnie, things that I really needed to remember. And that scared the hell out of me. Little Joe should have won the Classic. He was by far the best horse entered in that race. But I didn't give him the attention he needed and deserved that week, because all I could think about was you. Hell, when I woke up that morning all I wanted to do was lie there and look at you, and then wake you up and make love to you again. If I hadn't left when I did—the way I did—I might still be lying there in that bed with you, thinking about nothing else."

"And would that be so terrible?" she asked.

"Of course not," he told her. "But that wasn't why I was in Del Mar," he repeated. "I was in Del Mar to win a race. That was my job. And my work was the most important thing to me."

She said nothing for a moment, only studied his face in the darkness as if looking for the answer to a very important question. Finally she asked, "And what's the most important thing to you now, Daniel?"

Wasn't the answer to that obvious? "My work," he answered automatically.

She nodded slowly. "Of course," she said softly. "That is, after all, what you do best."

Her comment, too, puzzled him. She made it sound as if being good at what he did was a bad thing.

She bit her lip thoughtfully, her eyes fixed on his, glimmering in the scant moonlight that was filtering through the window. And damned if Daniel didn't find himself wanting to pull her into his arms and kiss her. But as much as it might have felt as if no time had passed since Del Mar, there were eight years between now and then. And eight years was a long time in the best of circumstances. For Daniel and Marnie, it was virtually a lifetime.

So Daniel turned and started for the door, then halted. He couldn't just walk away and leave things as they were, unsettled. He'd done that eight years ago and regretted it.

"It *was* good to see you again, Marnie," he said softly. And since he was being honest, he added, "I hope we see each other again."

She didn't say anything in response, only stood silhouetted against the window with her arms wrapped around her in a way that made him wonder whether she was doing it because she was cold, or if she just needed something—someone—to hold on to. In either case, Daniel understood. There was an emptiness clinging to him that he suspected would be there for a long time.

* * * * *

THOROUGHBRED LEGACY
coming soon wherever books are sold!

Harlequin Presents brings you
a brand-new duet by star author

Sharon Kendrick

THE GREEK BILLIONAIRES' BRIDES

Power, pride and passion—discover how only
the love and passion of two women can reunite
these wealthy, successful brothers,
divided by a bitter rivalry.

Available June 2008:

THE GREEK TYCOON'S
BABY BARGAIN

Available July 2008:

THE GREEK TYCOON'S
CONVENIENT WIFE

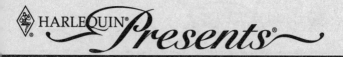

Don't miss the brilliant
new novel from

Natalie Rivers

**featuring a dark, dangerous
and decadent Italian!**

THE SALVATORE
MARRIAGE DEAL

Available June 2008
Book #2735

*Look out for more books
from Natalie Rivers coming soon,
only in Harlequin Presents!*

www.eHarlequin.com   HP12735

HARLEQUIN *Presents*

What do you look for in a guy?
Charisma. Sex appeal. Confidence.
A body to die for. Well, look no further
this series has men with all this and more!
And now that they've met the women in these novels,
there is one thing on everyone's mind....

NIGHTS *of* PASSION

One night is never enough!

**The guys know what they want
and how they're going to get it!**

Don't miss:

HIS MISTRESS
BY ARRANGEMENT
by
Natalie Anderson

Available June 2008.

*Look out for more Nights of Passion,
coming soon in Harlequin Presents!*

www.eHarlequin.com   HP12737

I ♥ HARLEQUIN *Presents*

BROUGHT TO YOU BY FANS OF
HARLEQUIN PRESENTS.

We are its editors and authors
and biggest fans—and we'd
love to hear from YOU!

Subscribe today to our online blog at
www.iheartpresents.com

HPBLOG

REQUEST YOUR FREE BOOKS!

HARLEQUIN *Presents*®

PASSION GUARANTEED SEDUCTION

2 FREE NOVELS
PLUS 2
FREE GIFTS!

YES! Please send me 2 FREE Harlequin Presents® novels and my 2 FREE gifts (gifts are worth about $10). After receiving them, if I don't wish to receive any more books, I can return the shipping statement marked "cancel". If I don't cancel, I will receive 6 brand-new novels every month and be billed just $4.05 per book in the U.S. or $4.74 per book in Canada, plus 25¢ shipping and handling per book and applicable taxes, if any*. That's a savings of close to 15% off the cover price! I understand that accepting the 2 free books and gifts places me under no obligation to buy anything. I can always return a shipment and cancel at any time. Even if I never buy another book, the two free books and gifts are mine to keep forever.

106 HDN ERRW   306 HDN ERRL

Name	(PLEASE PRINT)	
Address		Apt. #
City	State/Prov.	Zip/Postal Code

Signature (if under 18, a parent or guardian must sign)

Mail to the **Harlequin Reader Service:**
IN U.S.A.: P.O. Box 1867, Buffalo, NY 14240-1867
IN CANADA: P.O. Box 609, Fort Erie, Ontario L2A 5X3

Not valid to current subscribers of Harlequin Presents books.

Want to try two free books from another line?
Call 1-800-873-8635 or visit www.morefreebooks.com.

* Terms and prices subject to change without notice. N.Y. residents add applicable sales tax. Canadian residents will be charged applicable provincial taxes and GST. This offer is limited to one order per household. All orders subject to approval. Credit or debit balances in a customer's account(s) may be offset by any other outstanding balance owed by or to the customer. Please allow 4 to 6 weeks for delivery. Offer available while quantities last.

Your Privacy: Harlequin Books is committed to protecting your privacy. Our Privacy Policy is available online at www.eHarlequin.com or upon request from the Reader Service. From time to time we make our lists of customers available to reputable third parties who may have a product or service of interest to you. If you would prefer we not share your name and address, please check here. ☐

HP08

Don't forget Harlequin Presents EXTRA
now brings you a powerful new collection
every month featuring four books!

Be sure not to miss any of the titles in

In the Greek Tycoon's Bed,

available May 13:

THE GREEK'S FORBIDDEN BRIDE
by Cathy Williams

THE GREEK TYCOON'S UNEXPECTED WIFE
by Annie West

THE GREEK TYCOON'S VIRGIN MISTRESS
by Chantelle Shaw

THE GIANNAKIS BRIDE
by Catherine Spencer

www.eHarlequin.com

HPE0508

HARLEQUIN *Presents*

EXTRA

TALL, DARK AND SEXY

The men who never fail—seduction included!

Brooding, successful and arrogant, these men
can sweep any female they desire off her feet.
But now there's only one woman they want—
and they'll use their wealth, power, charm and
irresistibly seductive ways to claim her!

**Don't miss any of the titles in this exciting
collection available June 10, 2008:**

#9 THE BILLIONAIRE'S VIRGIN BRIDE
by HELEN BROOKS

#10 HIS MISTRESS BY MARRIAGE
by LEE WILKINSON

#11 THE BRITISH BILLIONAIRE AFFAIR
by SUSANNE JAMES

#12 THE MILLIONAIRE'S MARRIAGE REVENGE
by AMANDA BROWNING

*Harlequin Presents EXTRA delivers a themed
collection every month featuring 4 new titles.*

www.eHarlequin.com

HPE0608